CIRCUS O

Didi grimaced. Everythi ... She had sacrificed a lot ... dream—working with ele... in a circus. But in only two days' time it had turned into a real-life version of that terrible movie she'd seen so many times on late night TV: *Circus of Horrors*. And just for good measure, here she was being questioned by the state police.

She glared at Lieutenant Jacks. He only smiled gently at her.

"All right," she finally said, taking a huge breath. "Here is what happened. The management of the circus provided me with a pass because they wanted to hire me as a veterinary consultant for their two-week run. After Ti Nolan was killed, I vetted out the elephant. She seemed fine. That day was also the first and last time I saw the elephant's driver alive. You know the rest."

Lieutenant Jacks seemed to contemplate her words for a long time. "Do you have any idea what those letters mean—the ones written in blood on the walls . . . ?"

Dr. Nightingale Rides the Elephant

A DEIRDRE QUINN NIGHTINGALE MYSTERY

Lydia Adamson

A SIGNET BOOK

SIGNET
Published by the Penguin Group
Penguin Books USA Inc., 375 Hudson Street,
New York, New York 10014, U.S.A.
Penguin Books Ltd, 27 Wrights Lane,
London W8 5TZ, England
Penguin Books Australia Ltd, Ringwood,
Victoria, Australia
Penguin Books Canada Ltd, 10 Alcorn Avenue,
Toronto, Ontario, Canada M4V 3B2
Penguin Books (N.Z.) Ltd, 182–190 Wairau Road,
Auckland 10, New Zealand

Penguin Books Ltd, Registered Offices:
Harmondsworth, Middlesex, England

First published by Signet,
an imprint of Dutton Signet,
a division of Penguin Books USA Inc.

First Printing, August, 1994
10 9 8 7 6 5 4 3 2 1

The first chapter of this book previously appeared in
Dr. Nightingale Comes Home.

  REGISTERED TRADEMARK—MARCA REGISTRADA

Printed in the United States of America

PUBLISHER'S NOTE
This is a work of fiction. Names, characters, places, and incidents either
are the product of the author's imagination or are used fictitiously, and any
resemblance to actual persons, living or dead, events, or locales is entirely
coincidental.

Chapter 1

It was simply too cold that February morning to sit on the bare ground, so Didi placed a piece of cardboard down and then assumed the lotus position to begin her daily yogic breathing.

Her heart, however, wasn't in her exercises that morning. And it wasn't only because of the cold. She was going to the circus!

There would be no veterinary work today. No rounds. No clinic. No goats with sexual problems. No horses cast in their stall. No dogs with ticks. No cows with stringy milk.

Didi dearly loved being a veterinarian. But she loved the circus more. Even at twenty-eight she still had a child's enthusiasm for the Big Top.

She wasn't going to the Ringling Bros. and Barnum & Bailey Circus in Madison Square Garden, where her mother had taken her every year from the age of four on.

No, this was a small one-ring traveling circus that was setting up on the grounds of what had once been Sennett College, on the outskirts of

Hillsbrook—equidistant, in fact, from the three towns of Rhinebeck, Poughkeepsie, and Hillsbrook.

And the trip wasn't sheerly for pleasure. The circus people wanted to interview her for the job of veterinarian-in-residence during their twenty-day run. For Didi, a chance to be near Asian elephants again was a gift from the gods.

Didi grimaced when she realized that Sara, the Spotted Poland China Sow, was taking an intense interest in the breathing exercises. She was staring at Didi with those intense pig eyes from between the slats of the farrowing pen. According to the 114-day cycle, Sara was due to give birth in three days.

Didi had known the pig problem would eventually get out of hand. She should have stopped it when she first came back to Hillsbrook . . . when she came home to practice veterinary medicine in farm country, where she had grown up.

But Didi had come home to find herself heir to a quartet of "retainers"—Charlie Gravis, Mrs. Tunney, Trent Tucker, and Abigail. All her mother's loyal employees were now, crazily, for better or worse, under Didi's reluctant protection.

All four swore that the pigs were family pets who had been much loved by Didi's mother. Of course, they had lied. Each autumn, the quartet slaughtered two of the hogs—the so-called family pets—no matter what Didi said. They ate most of the meat and sold the rest. And Didi had never dared to stop it, although she constantly complained. She really didn't mind their selling the meat—after all, they received no wages from her, only room and board in the big house. It was the slaughter she couldn't handle.

What with the cold and the staring sow and her thoughts of the circus—she did a very abbreviated breathing routine and then ran into the house. Mrs. Tunney was preparing her signature breakfast dish: oatmeal. Charlie Gravis, Didi's geriatric veterinary assistant, was seated at the table along with Abigail and young Trent Tucker. They were all bundled up against the chill.

Didi announced the schedule to them. "We'll leave about ten-thirty. The matinee starts at noon and Mr. Allenbach has left tickets for all of us. I have to meet with him at about eleven-fifteen. We'll take the jeep. It'll be a close fit but we can all get in."

She waited for their joyous response. They huddled over their bowls, waiting for the magical oatmeal Mrs. Tunney was stirring in her enormous kettle. Even the ethereal, golden-haired Abigail looked grim. And Trent Tucker, who usually had a quip for every occasion, seemed to be contemplating the contours of his spoon.

Who can deal with these people, Didi thought, and strode angrily out of the kitchen, through the hallway, up the stairs, and into her mother's old bedroom. She flung herself down on the bed to brood.

They all left in Didi's red jeep promptly at ten-thirty, a solid mass of parkas, scarves, fur-lined boots, and mittens.

Didi played Patsy Cline tapes all the way there. Abigail and Trent Tucker hummed along. Charlie Gravis pouted—he did not like Patsy. Mrs. Tunney seemed not to be hearing the music at all.

What an odd group we are, Didi thought. Dr. Didi Quinn Nightingale, DVM, and her four elves.

They arrived at the old Sennett College site at 11:00 A.M. sharp. A huge tent had been set up with a banner proclaiming the name of the circus, THE ORIGINAL DALTON'S BIG TOP CIRCUS, and the dates of the performances.

Behind the tent was the semicircle of mobile homes where the circus performers lived.

And behind these were four large trailer trucks, one of which had cages on a flatbed. It was obvious that this small circus did not tour via Amtrak.

Didi went alone to the small mobile home that also functioned as an administrative office. The manager, Thomas Allenbach, was seated on a large carton, eating a turkey sandwich and sipping from a bottle of soda. He was a young man in his early thirties, with longish sandy hair and a well-trimmed beard. He wore a muffler and a hiking vest.

"Can I help you?" he asked brightly.

"I'm Dr. Nightingale," she said.

He stared at her, wide-eyed. He didn't answer. She waited. Then he put his sandwich down.

"I'm sorry. I'm sorry. It's just that you surprised me. I never expected the vet I would be interviewing would be so pretty and so young."

"Well, I think you're pretty, too," Didi retorted, trying to nip this kind of nonsense in the bud. It worked. He got right to the point.

"You were recommended to us highly. It's a twenty-day run here and we need someone to stop in at least once a day and check the animals out. And to be on call if anything happens."

"It's also state law," Didi reminded him.

"I'm aware of that," he said, smiling.

"Could you tell me who recommended me?" She was genuinely curious.

He grinned wider and said, "I don't reveal my sources." Then he added: "But they did tell me that Didi Nightingale knows elephants."

Didi felt uncomfortable. The unnamed source who recommended her must have known that after vet school she had spent a year in Madras with Dr. Mohandas Medawar, probably the most respected researcher in the world in the realm of Asian elephants. But the same source probably did not know that she really hadn't done any real clinical, hands-on work while there. Medawar was conducting an ambitious study under the auspices of the Fund For Animals. Teams were being sent all over Asia to locate, count, and describe the conditions of elephants still used for work. Didi had been assigned to the team that wandered through Laos, Cambodia, Thailand, and Vietnam. It had been exciting . . . often dangerous . . . and she had seen many elephants up close, but she had rarely treated one. In Southwest Asian logging camps the *mahouts* have their own medicines.

No . . . she couldn't claim to "know" Asian elephants. But should she admit that fact to Allenbach?

Allenbach interpreted her silence as modesty. He continued. "So here's what we got. Five Asian elephants. All females. Three Bengal tigers. Two female and one male. And the Shetland ponies. That's it. The animals are in excellent condition."

For the first time Didi noticed that the walls of the mobile home were lined with political campaign buttons of all kinds from all eras. She could make out Clinton and Gore, Reagan and Bush, Mondale and Ferraro, FDR, Dewey, Willkie, and a host of others.

"And the pay, Dr. Nightingale, is $280 a week," he said picking up his sandwich once again.

"Are you serious?" Didi shot back, astonished at the ridiculously low figure. She had expected a sum closer to $2,800 a week. It was a lot of work and a lot of responsibility.

"I'm afraid that's all we can afford."

"Well, thank you for the interview and the free tickets, Mr. Allenbach. But count me out." She started to walk out of the trailer.

"Wait!" Allenbach put the remainder of his lunch down again. "Don't take the low offer as a personal insult. That's what we pay. If you expected more you have no understanding of what circuses are about now. We don't make money anymore. Even the big ones. Understand. The circus world is for the fools . . . the romantics . . . or those who just love a very old and very beautiful way of life and way of performing.

"The only reason my company keeps on going is because when the Soviet Union collapsed, all the great circus performers in Eastern Europe—and that's where the great acrobats and jugglers and clowns always were—started to come to the U.S. They came in waves and they worked for peanuts. Get it, Dr. Nightingale? That offer I made to you . . . which you considered an insult . . . is the highest weekly wage in this circus."

"You made your point. Now let me make mine. If I agree to your offer it means essentially I have to abandon my practice for three weeks. And I need an income to replace that because I'm simply not independently wealthy. I work for a living. I have bills to pay. I have a large house and a lot of people who depend on me. It would have been very nice, Mr. Allenbach. I love circuses. I love circus animals. But I simply can't afford your salary."

She walked over to him and extended her hand. He took it. "Why don't you go to the matinee, Dr. Nightingale, and enjoy the show? Think it over. Call me one way or the other after six this evening. Okay?" He gave Didi his card and she walked out.

Once inside the Big Top, Didi spotted her "elves" seated way up in the wooden school-gymnasium-type bleachers that lined both sides of the tent. The four of them looked happy. They were all stuffing themselves with cotton candy or hot dogs or candied apples or popcorn. It was slow going for Didi as she made her way up and through the aisles to join the crew: the stands were now packed with parents and children.

Didi had barely sat down when the lights dimmed and the ringmaster in top hat entered the center of the ring. An all-American brass band started up. Didi looked around. Where was the band? Then she saw a single man in a lighted alcove playing with the controls of a flashing board like the music mixer in a disco. The brass band was canned and computer generated.

Two clowns ran out into the ring and to the delight of the audience kept interfering with the ringmaster's announcement. Finally, it was time for the opening parade. The "band" switched to a version of "Hail to the Chief" and each of the circus stars made his or her appearance, running across the ring and then vanishing out the other side.

First came the Shelty Sisters—five "little people" with the nine Shetland ponies on which they performed their acrobatic feats.

Then came The Great Zappanus in their sequins and capes—the formerly great high wire artists who now merely performed unbelievable somersaults.

Then the world-famous Lothar Strauss and his

three dazzling Bengal tigers, roaring as they were pulled across the ring in their cage.

Finally the fire swallower, Laz Runay—direct!, according to the announcer, from the renowned Hungarian State Circus.

The lights went out completely and a hush settled over the crowd. Didi knew what was about to happen. The elephants were coming. She felt like a six-year-old kid . . . happy . . . anticipatory . . . did she love elephants!

"Ladies and Gentlemen . . . " the announcer hawked. "Direct from the steaming jungles of Asia, I bring you Tran Van Minh and his beautiful beasts . . . Lutzi and Gorgeous and Alma and Dolly . . . and the great Queen."

A drum roll. A barrage of spotlights and out trotted the first elephant, ridden by the trainer Tran Van Minh. She was a beautiful elephant, bedecked with red and gold trappings.

Behind her marched another awesome beast, this one's trunk holding the first one's tail.

Alma, Dolly, and Queen each carried a dancing girl who began to pirouette wildly the moment her elephant reached the center of the ring. The applause and shouts were deafening.

The elephants pranced out the far side of the tent.

All eyes went back to the center of the ring, where the ringmaster held his enormous whip high in the air.

And then, suddenly, there seemed to be a collective gasp . . . a kind of astonishment from one part of the bleachers.

Didi turned toward the exit. One of the elephants was backing up into the ring, much to the delight of the audience. The children began to cheer. When she was all the way back, she wheeled suddenly and the dancing girl tumbled off the elephant's back, hitting the ground hard about five feet from her mount.

The elephant ambled over to the little dancer, placed her front foot on the head of the fallen girl, and crushed her to death.

Chapter 2

Dolly stood placidly, tethered to the ground, only a few feet away from the bloodstained spot where she had killed the dancing girl. She seemed to be unconcerned . . . not to be suffering from the slightest twinge of guilt or remorse or fear. The elephant seemed at ease.

All the spectators had been sent home with rain checks for the next afternoon's matinee. The ambulance and the state police cars had also left with the corpse. The circus performers huddled together near the ring exit, still in their costumes, chattering nervously.

Didi's "elves" remained high in the stands, alone. Charlie Gravis had fallen fast asleep. Mrs. Tunney was knitting. Trent Tucker was fiddling with his Walkman. And Abigail, as usual, was lost in some reverie.

At the edge of the ring, watching Dolly, stood Thomas Allenbach, the elephant handler Tran Van Minh, and Didi. Across the ring, on the far edge, stood a solitary state trooper and the man who made the circus music on a computerized sound system—Alfred Faulkner. Both held high-powered rifles with scopes, ready if Dolly made another aggressive move.

The waves of horror kept surfacing in Didi's head. It was a visual memory—a lovely young woman's skull being crushed by that awesome gray column of flesh and muscle. It was different from any other trauma Didi had ever witnessed and she had seen much in her short professional life as a vet. From horses impaled during jumping contests to cows gored by bulls in abortive breeding attempts. Yes, this had been something else altogether. She kept fighting to keep her poise, to maintain a professional stance. All the faces around her were ashen, no matter the degree of poise. She wondered what she looked like now.

Then Tran started to shake his head violently from side to side. He looked at Allenbach and then at Didi. "She is the gentlest of them all," he said, his painfully thin body taut, his fists punching out to accentuate his belief. His English was very good, if stilted. He's Vietnamese, Didi thought. Tran had a dark black cowlick. He might have been twenty. He might have been forty.

"Well, it happened," Allenbach said, a bit sardonically.

"She is a good kind lady," Tran said. "The kindest of them all. She understands everything."

"Sure," Allenbach said. "She's so kind she cracked that girl's head like an eggshell." Then he said to Didi in an imploring voice: "Can you take a look at her, Dr. Nightingale?"

Didi knew what he was asking. The people from the state agency would be there shortly. Allenbach needed a vet to certify that it was just an accident, that Dolly was not dangerous . . . that she should not be destroyed. Didi didn't answer for a long while. She really didn't know where her responsibility lay. She hadn't accepted or refused the proffered position yet, and, if anything, she had been leaning toward refusing the job. At least before the horrible incident had occurred. She just couldn't work for that kind of money.

She stared at Dolly, standing so quietly, and then past her, to the two men with weapons.

"Okay," she finally said. Then she turned to Tran. "Any sign of *musth*?" She used the native term for rut or estrous: a condition which in many elephants causes them to turn aggressive. It was a state much feared in the logging camps she had visited.

"No—no *musth*!" Tran said. Then he repeated it even more fiercely: "No *musth*!" He turned to Didi then and ordered, "Smell her!"

"What is he talking about?" Allenbach asked angrily.

Didi explained. "An elephant in the state called *musth*, which may or may not stem from estrous or rut, secretes a foul-smelling substance from the temporal gland between the eye and the ear. It always signifies stress, and with stress comes aggression."

"Then do as he says. Smell her!"

Didi did not like the way he'd said it. As if he were ordering her about. She wanted to bring him down a peg somehow. "You know," she said, "it doesn't really matter what I find. The state people are going to make their own examination and they're going to require you to isolate her. If Dolly does survive, it'll be a long time before you can put her back to work as a circus performer."

Allenbach raised his hands in a form of apology for his brusqueness. Then Didi nodded to Tran and the two of them walked slowly toward the tethered beast.

Dolly watched them as they approached her. Didi felt a growing anticipation: It wasn't fear. It was more a kind of awe. And then she was right up on the magnificent beast.

Happy to see Tran, Dolly began to sway ever so slightly, and he scratched her under her left front foot. Didi's eyes roamed quickly over the huge animal. Nothing seemed amiss. The eyes were clear, the skin cool to the touch. The trunk fell freely and gently. The ears were not flared. Didi caught her breath; she truly loved these beasts. She always had and always would. She had to remind herself that Dolly was a killer.

She stepped away from the elephant, but not too far back. There was no hint of the *musth* odor. Not a trace of that distinct smell, which can best be described as sweet and sour twine being burned.

Didi inhaled and exhaled as if performing one of her yogic exercises. She had to be sure. Dolly swung her trunk toward Didi as if reaching out for her. Didi wanted very much to scratch the huge thing—and Dolly was indeed a huge female Asian elephant. She stood a bit over ten feet and probably weighed close to three tons. The tethers anchoring her to the floor of the ring would tear like so much tissue paper if Dolly chose to break them.

Didi heard Tran speak to the elephant, this time in an Asian tongue. The elephant raised one foot tentatively off the ground. Didi's professional demeanor dissolved instantly. She had a sudden fantasy that the elephant was going to kneel and that she, Didi, would climb up on Dolly's back and ride around the ring performing a daring routine. Didi blushed at her foolishness and came back to reality.

"Dolly wants to play with you," Tran said in English. Didi gave him a disgusted look, turned on her heel and walked back to the anxiously waiting Thomas Allenbach.

"She looks calm," he said.

"She is calm. Almost too calm. And there is no sign of the *musth*. But, as I said, the state authorities will conduct their own investigation and they will use their own vets."

"Can we take a walk together for a moment?" he asked, his voice containing a note of mystery. Didi followed him outside. It was very cold. Allenbach obviously didn't really want to walk, only to talk. "Listen," he began, "we need you now more than ever. We need a good vet for the rest of the run. So people can trust us. After all, they know you. I don't want people to think all our animals are killers. We won't fill any seats."

Didi shook her head. "I told you I just can't afford that kind of salary."

"But it wouldn't require that much time out of your day unless something happens. We're talking about an hour or two. Why don't you just keep working at your practice while you're taking care of our animals?"

She shook her head sadly, as if his words were too stupid to bear.

"Did I say something wrong?"

Again, she didn't reply. Poor Thomas Allenbach. He was a young man, she thought, but he sounded just like old Charlie Gravis. Allenbach had the old-fashioned view of veterinarians: If a horse is colicky, just put a tube down its mouth with some kind of medicinal brew and then come back the next day. If the horse is alive, fine. If it's dead, sad. But colic could be a result of anything from improper diet to anatomic displacement of the colon to ulceration of the GI tract. To find out and to prescribe properly, you had to stay with the animal and run tests, all kinds of tests. You simply couldn't be a good vet anymore with regular rounds and then take on a potentially time-consuming job like the circus. It was one or the other.

A sudden gust of wind half spun Didi around. She heard Allenbach say something else, but she couldn't make out the words."

"What did you say?"

"Ti Nolan."

The words meant nothing to Didi. "Who?"

"I said that the dancing girl's name was Ti Nolan. The dead girl. Her name was Ti Nolan."

And then the horror came back to Didi . . . the horror of what she had seen and heard earlier . . . a head cracking open like a walnut shell . . . blood . . . screams. And for some reason, however murky, there was no longer any question. All her logical arguments against taking the job evaporated. "I'll take the job," she said. "I'll drop by the first thing in the morning."

Then she went back to the big tent to collect her elves.

Chapter 3

Allie Voegler woke from his stolen nap in his unmarked police car. He rubbed his eyes and slowly rotated his creaky stiff neck.

Then he turned to roll down the window to get some cold air on his face.

Another face loomed up suddenly from outside the car . . . a face so horrible that Allie shrank back involuntarily and fumbled for his service revolver lying in its holster on the seat next to him.

Then he realized it was only a dog. John Theobold's goofy Lab/Bloodhound mix, Bucket. The dog had shoved his enormous snout through the half-open window.

"Damn you, Bucket! What are you doing here? You're two miles from home."

Bucket just whined and kept trying to enter the car through the window.

"What the hell do you want, dog?" Allie shouted at him. "Why don't you get your ugly nose out of my vehicle?" But then Allie noticed the forgotten, now stale cruller on the dashboard. "You really want that, Bucket?"

The dog groaned deeply.

Allie grabbed the cruller, opened the door and flung the stale pastry onto the ground about five feet away from the car. Bucket trotted over, plopped down and started to chew contentedly.

Allie stepped out of the car and stretched. It was cold in the early morning sun. He watched Bucket chew for a while. Then Allie grinned. What a menace that fool dog was. Constantly getting into trouble. Oh, not bad trouble. He didn't kill deer, he didn't steal chickens. But he was always colliding with a kid on a bike or causing untold complications in his pursuit of a simple bone or tin can. If there was any mess to fall into, Bucket would find it. And the one who always fixed him up was none other than Dr. Didi Quinn Nightingale. In fact, Bucket was probably Didi's best client. That hound's adventures always ended on the vet's table.

At the thought of Didi Q. Nightingale, Allie's smile vanished. He wasn't doing too well on that front. She didn't want to marry him . . . she didn't want to sleep with him . . . she didn't want to eat supper with him. All she seemed to want to do with him was go to the movies . . . once in a while.

Voegler shook his head. After he and Didi had worked together so closely in solving the murder of her friend Dick Obey, he thought it would be different.

Bucket started moaning again. He wanted another cruller.

"Bad break hit you," Allie said. "That's all I have, hound." And then he had a delicious idea.

Allie looked at his watch. It was about six-thirty. Didi would be performing her ridiculous breathing exercises just about this time of morning, out behind her house, while those characters who sponged off her sat in a warm kitchen stuffing their faces with Didi's food. What if he brought Bucket around to see her? What if he told her that Bucket had sought out his wise counsel, but Allie decided to bring the hound in to a real vet. Yeah, it would be a good joke.

Allie straightened up, a little embarrassed at his plan. He was going to greater and greater lengths to see Didi, clutching at any opportunity. He weighed the advantages and disadvantages of his joke. Then he opened the rear door of the car and called to Bucket, who lumbered happily onto the seat and draped his drooling muzzle over the top of the front seat.

Allie's plan was aborted halfway to Didi's place by a radio call: there had been a break-in at Charles Dunlop's home on Wright Lane. Allie dropped Bucket off about a hundred yards from the gate to his master's dairy farm, one of the few remaining in that section of Dutchess County, and then he made a dramatic U turn and headed back in the other direction at high speed.

The Hillsbrook Police cruiser was already

parked in the driveway of the spacious Dunlop house. Charles Dunlop was the vice president of Hillsbrook Savings & Loan and had lived in the house all his life, as had his parents before him.

As Allie pushed the half-open door back he could see how the burglars had entered. They had simply smashed in one of the stained-glass front windows, reached in and unlocked it. Primitive but effective. In the living room, Officer Storch greeted Allie deferentially; Allie was the only plainclothes detective on Hillsbrook's eight-person police force, and thus commanded respect.

"The trash man forgot that Dunlop and his wife were away. He came to pick up, found the window smashed, the door open, and stuff scattered all over the grounds," Storch reported.

"What stuff?"

Storch pointed to a pile of objects on the living-room rug. "I brought them in. The kids who did this must have been so soused they dropped whatever they stole on the way to their pickup. I got a feeling, Allie, that they were just looking for a place to drink, so they came in here, got loaded, then started pulling anything they thought they could sell out of the house."

Voegler nodded. The room was also littered with crushed beer cans, and here and there lay the empties of what looked to have been really bad bourbon.

"What about the rest of the house?" Allie asked.

"They ransacked the chests in the two bedrooms, probably took silver and jewelry, looks like. We'll have to wait till Dunlop gets back to give us a list."

Allie sat down on a brocaded chair and took a measured look around the room. It was as if a herd of buffalo had been driven through the place. Along with the smell of stale booze was the stench of urine. One of the intruders must have used the fireplace.

It was a beautiful room, Allie thought, even after the buffalo. For a moment he speculated what it might be like to live in such a house— with Didi Nightingale. Yes, that would be very nice.

Along the walls were a series of paintings of hunting dogs, all obviously by the same artist. A spaniel hunting quail . . . a setter retrieving a duck . . . a pack of Airedales treeing a mountain lion. On either side of the paintings there hung on high open racks a group of shotguns with beautifully inlaid stocks.

On the wall opposite the fireplace was a reproduction of a deerskin map made by Comanche Indians circa 1840. And next to it was a single large photograph of Dunlop and his wife taken several years ago aboard a sailing boat.

Allie was bounced out of his reverie of money and class by Officer Storch's exclamation. "Damn, look at this! It's a damn shame."

Storch had pulled up a long glass case from behind one of the living room tables. "It must have been hanging on one of the walls," he said.

Allie looked down into the splintered mess. The big glass box contained five intricate moorings for five fishing rods, but now only three of the rods were left. Each was secured inside the case as lovingly as a baby picture in a silver frame.

"Why keep fishing rods in a thing like that?" Allie asked. "Like they were museum pieces?"

"Cause they're antique fly rods, Allie, that's why." Storch had obviously been transported. There was a look of sheer bliss on his face. Tenderly he brought out one of the poles and flicked it expertly. "Whew! Never thought I'd live to hold one of these. It must be worth thousands. Must be over a hundred years old."

"Who collects this kind of thing?"

"Are you kidding?" Storch asked contemptuously and pulled the case away from Allie as if he were no longer worthy of gazing at it.

"Will they be able to get rid of it quickly?" Allie asked.

"They took two," Storch corrected. "And I don't know. You could sell it to a collector in a minute, I suppose. But won't a collector be a little suspicious when some scruffy kid calls him up on the phone and wants to meet him in an alley somewhere and says he'll only take cash?"

"Where do you find collectors?"

"The Classified section of the fishing magazines. Damn, Allie, don't you read anymore?"

Allie decided it would be prudent not to answer. He sat back and shut his eyes, signaling to Storch that the conversation was over and it was about time he got back to work. There was furniture to "dust," reports to fill out, photos to take. Storch went out to the cruiser to get his kit.

Allie was tired. He couldn't think much now. It was hard luck to catch a breaking-and-entering at the end of a shift. Difficult to make the right connections. Everything blurred together—the brick that broke the window dissolved into the silver tray, which dissolved into the empty beer can. His eyes still closed, he wondered how Bucket was doing. He wondered if Didi had finished her exercises, and whether they had gone particularly well this particular morning—though he hadn't the foggiest idea what those strange breathing exercises were supposed to do for her. She was already so damn handsome she didn't need any exercises.

Allie stood up quickly, almost violently, suddenly ashamed of falling into a dumb dream state at a crime scene. His eye fell upon the dog paintings again. For a moment he had the bizarre thought that the same artist who painted the canvases on Dunlop's wall was at this moment heading toward John Theobold's farm to do a painting of that great hunting dog Bucket.

Jesus! Allie thought—smiling in spite of himself—this thing with Didi is sending me around the bend. His eyes then went to the beautiful shotguns displayed on the wall. He liked guns. He liked hunting. But he despised fishing. Putting a bullet through a deer's heart at three hundred yards after stalking the buck for five hours and killing him instantly seemed fine to Allie. But he couldn't abide fishing. That seemed the ultimate cruelty. Decoying the fish with a lure, hooking it savagely, and then pulling it out of the water and letting it die of asphyxiation in the air. Didi had said his views were inconsistent, contradictory. The two of them had argued about it. Well, weren't they always fighting about something—the few times they saw each other?

He sat down on the arm of the overstuffed chair and stared hard at the exquisite shotguns. And then realized something was funny . . . wrong . . . about this break-in. Was there ever a soused kid who didn't go for a gun? Didn't half the killings in the world start with the deadly combination of a kid with too much booze in him and all too easy access to a gun? Why were these kids any different?

But according to Storch, they had broken in to get out of the cold and party—the robbery had been almost an afterthought. They had seen all these goodies and decided to load up their truck with anything convertible. So why not the guns? How could they have missed those expensive shotguns, there for the plucking, and taken some antique fishing rods that would be almost impossible to fence? Any kind of gun was cash on the hoof.

Allie kicked the toe of his boot rhythmically against the burled coffee table. Yes, there was definitely something funny about this one.

Chapter 4

Didi spent the entire morning on the day after she had accepted the circus assignment making contingency plans with other vets in the area to cover her clients.

Around noon she asked Charlie to tell the others there would be a "staff" meeting in the kitchen in an hour.

When Didi entered the huge kitchen area, about three minutes after one, the staff had assembled, minus Abigail.

Mrs. Tunney was serving her cold weather specialty: cocoa. She made it the same way every time. Mix coffee, cocoa, cinnamon, and honey with a little hot water at the bottom of a large pot until a paste has formed. Then heat milk in another pot and pour the hot milk over the paste.

Didi sat down at the long kitchen table. Mrs. Tunney poured her a mug and slid it toward her. Didi recoiled in involuntary disgust. The top of the cocoa was covered with milk skin and Didi could not stand even looking at it.

"Why do you always boil the milk until there's gook on top, Mrs. Tunney?"

"It's good for you," she replied brightly. Trent Tucker and Charlie Gravis both nodded their heads in agreement.

Didi bowed her head. Why did she always fall into the trap? It was futile to argue with *them*. They had been more or less willed to her by her mother. She was honor bound to take care of them, and she would. But it was futile trying to reason with them.

Mrs. Tunney thought she was the absolute Queen of Hausfraus. Charlie Gravis thought every surgical and pharmaceutical breakthrough in veterinary science was inferior to his herbal remedies. Young Tucker thought he was the coolest dude in Dutchess County. In fact, Didi didn't even know what Trent Tucker did, other than take care of the furnaces and the shifting population of dogs and cats that made the perimeter of the Nightingale house their home.

As for Abigail . . . she was on another planet.

"Where is Abigail?" Didi asked.

Mrs. Tunney looked at her archly. "With Sara, miss. Where she is supposed to be."

Didi had forgotten all about the pregnant sow. Now she decided to forget about Abigail and get on with the meeting.

"We are all going to have to pull together during the next few weeks," she began. "To be honest, I don't know why I accepted the job, but I did. And Charlie and I are going to do the very best we can." She paused, contemplating how much of herself to reveal. "Maybe I took it because of that terrible thing we all witnessed yesterday. Or maybe because I feel an obligation to the girl who died. Or it could be that I'm just a sucker for elephants. Anyway, the important thing is to take care of our clients when I'm at the circus. On my office desk I taped the numbers of three vets who will be covering for me if anything comes up. Just answer all calls and refer where you think necessary. Please don't give any advice over the phone. Tell them who to call. If they ask where I am, tell them I took a short vacation." She smiled. "I sure deserve one. Any questions?"

"What about Sara?" Trent Tucker asked.

"This isn't her first litter. And if she's late we'll give her an injection," Didi replied tartly, then marched into her office to get her supplies ready, signaling for Charlie to follow.

Together they loaded two large satchels with pain killers, tranquilizers, muscle relaxers, antibiotics, medicinal washes, gauze, syringes, sponges, scalpels, surgical thread, splints, and a lot more. Didi had no idea what she would need, so she took just about everything she had to spare. She would set up an infirmary on the circus grounds.

When that task was finished, Didi started searching through her files of veterinary magazines and her bookshelves.

She knew a great deal about Shetland ponies.

She knew a respectable amount about elephants.

But she knew absolutely nothing about the care of Bengal tigers. And that was the kind of information she was trying to dig up. What she found, alas, could be slipped into a single air mail envelope.

The day seemed to evaporate. She felt as if she'd been working since sunup without a single break. Didi fell into bed at nine, giving not a thought to the fact that she'd had no dinner.

They left in the red jeep at six-thirty the next morning. To cheer up a grumpy Charlie, Didi bought him breakfast—pancakes and bacon.

They reached the circus grounds just past 8:00 A.M. Didi parked the jeep in front of the administrative trailer.

The sounds of an ugly argument burst upon them the moment she turned off the ignition.

Thomas Allenbach was yelling at someone. At first she didn't recognize the other man, but then she realized it was the tiger trainer, Lothar Strauss.

Allenbach had calmed down but she could hear quite distinctly what he was saying. "All I want you to do is lead the elephants out of the trucks and feed and water them in the closed ring. Is that so much? It'll take you ten minutes." His voice, in fact, had become pleading.

"I *don't* feed elephants," Strauss replied. "Where is Tran?"

"I told you, I don't know where he is! Maybe he's off drunk somewhere. Maybe he left in the middle of the night. I don't know!"

Then Allenbach noticed Didi as she sat watching the proceedings. He walked quickly over and apologized. "I'm afraid you're seeing us at our worst," he said.

"I can take the elephants out," she offered.

He looked at her, startled, and then seemed to be seriously contemplating the offer when suddenly a small, powerfully built man in a hooded sweatshirt bounded up. "You want me?" he asked Allenbach.

Didi recognized him as one of the Zappanus—the trapeze artists.

"Yes. We have to get into Tran's trailer. Where is he? Sick? Drunk? Did he pull out? We have to get inside . . . understand?"

The acrobat led the way to the trailer followed by Allenbach, Lothar Strauss, Didi, and a grumbling Charlie Gravis.

When they reached the trailer, Zappanu seemed to know exactly what to do, as if this were a common occurrence in traveling troupes.

He grabbed an umbrella, shimmied up a drainpipe, kicked open a transom, stretched his arm down and opened the door latch from the inside with the umbrella's handle

The trailer door swung open.

Allenbach strode in angrily. Seconds later he staggered out jerkily. Lothar Strauss grabbed him before he could fall.

Didi, not thinking, rushed past him into the trailer.

Tran Van Minh was seated on the small pull-down sofa in the alcove.

The floor and his pants and the sofa were covered with blood.

He had slit his wrists lengthwise with a straight razor. And his forearms. And his chest.

On the wall behind him he had tried to write something—apparently in his own blood—before he died.

It looked as if he had written the letters S . . . I . . . R . . . I

Didi came out of the trailer very slowly, walked ten feet away from the door, and crouched in a fetal position near the ground until the nausea passed.

Chapter 5

"They're going to close us down! They are going to close us down!" one of the little people—one of the Shelty sisters—kept repeating over and over in a near hysterical voice. All five of the sisters were seated in the stands in the main ring, dressed in bathrobes and mufflers and identical fur-lined boots. They were all in hair curlers.

Almost the entire personnel roster of the circus was spread out behind them, like members of a tour group trying to pretend they didn't know one another.

Only one circus performer was not in the stands. That was the fire swallower, Laz. He was in the center of the ring being interrogated by a state trooper in plainclothes, a uniformed colleague at his side.

Everyone in the stands was waiting his or her turn to be questioned, including Didi. She didn't mind the sitting, the waiting. She hadn't fully recovered from what she had seen.

In fact, the chatter around her was oddly soothing even though many of the chatterers seemed poised at the edge of lunacy. After all, the performers had watched one of their number get crushed to death in an instant. And thirty-six hours later another of them had sliced himself apart in the most horrifying fashion. No wonder they were all talking nonsense . . . if they could talk at all.

Thomas Allenbach slid into the seat next to Didi. "We have a new elephant handler flying down from Montreal this afternoon. His name is Pak Pavala. Cambodian, I think. Would you help him get acclimated? I mean, just stay with him for a while."

"You work fast," Didi noted, a trace of censure in her voice.

Allenbach bristled. "Without a handler, this circus folds immediately. Don't you understand that! Or are you blaming me for what happened with Tran? I didn't know he was depressed, let alone suicidal. You saw him after the accident. He was fine. What was I supposed to do—hire a shrink as well as a vet?"

He pointed angrily toward the center of the ring, where the police milled. "They have no right to be doing this . . . questioning us like we were criminals. Animals go berserk. People, too. They commit suicide. That's the way of the world."

Didi did not respond to his outburst right away. What could she say? Someone about five rows down waved tentatively at her. It was one of the other dancing girls. Didi smiled weakly back at her.

Then she said to Allenbach: "I think it's a matter of public safety, that's all. Whatever the reason, two of your performing artists died violently within forty-eight hours. The police have a responsibility to the public. They have to do . . . they have to do something."

Allenbach sighed and then gave Didi a disgusted look, as if he were suddenly aware of what a fool he was to confide in a total stranger to circus life, a rube. He remained in his seat, silent, waiting along with everyone else.

A few minutes later Faulkner, the music man, joined him. He looked weary. He did not greet Didi.

Laz Runay came back to the stands. The Great Zappanus headed toward the interrogation spot— all six of them—as a group. They walked out flamboyantly, as if this, too, were a performance. The moment the fire swallower sat down he started whispering into the tiger trainer's ear.

Didi realized that her shock was wearing off. She was getting impatient. She was a consulting veterinarian, not a circus performer. And she had not known the dead dancer or the elephant handler.

At last the uniformed trooper with the clipboard called out her name. Didi strode to the folding table and sat down in the metal chair provided. She was growing warn, so she pulled open the snaps of her fleece-lined denim jacket.

"I'm Lieutenant Jacks," said the plainclothes officer. "I won't keep you long. I understand you just hired on."

"That's correct."

"And your full name?"

"Deidre Quinn Nightingale, D.V.M."

"Do you live in the area?"

"Hillsbrook."

Lieutenant Jacks nodded in a kindly fashion. He was, in fact, kindly in appearance and speech, more like a junior high counselor than a cop. He wore a knit tie on a flannel shirt. Didi liked the combination; it reminded her of how her literature professors used to dress in winter. Jacks was a shortish man with very wide shoulders and a thick neck. His hair was gray and clipped short.

"Could you tell us what your relationship was with Tran Van Minh . . . if any."

It was such a curious question that Didi asked, without thinking, really, "Then you think he was murdered. That it wasn't a suicide at all."

The two state troopers looked at each other. Lieutenant Jacks said, "We have no reason to suspect homicide." He paused for a minute, watching her face, and then went on: "Can you tell us how you knew Tran Van Minh?"

Didi grimaced. Everything had become absurd. She had sacrificed a lot financially to realize a dream—working with elephants in a circus. But, in only two days' time, it had turned into the real life version of that terrible movie she'd seen so many times on late night TV while she was away at school: *Circus of Horrors*. And just for good measure, here she was being questioned by the state police.

She glared at the lieutenant. Jacks only smiled gently at her.

"All right," she finally said, taking a huge breath. "Here is what happened: I came here to the matinee two days ago. The management of the circus provided me with a pass because they wanted to hire me as a veterinary consultant for their three-week run here. That was the afternoon Ti Nolan was killed, during the opening parade. After the accident I vetted out the elephant. She seemed fine. That day was also the first and the last time I saw Tran alive. He was upset, of course, but perfectly rational. Sure, he was trying to defend his charge. He knew her survival was at stake. But he certainly did not look like a man twenty-four hours away from suicide. I did not come to the circus grounds yesterday. I arrived this morning about eight with my assistant and several cases of supplies. The first person I encountered was Mr. Allenbach. You know the rest."

Jacks seemed to contemplate her words for a long time. "Do you have any idea what those letters meant—the ones written in blood on the wall?"

"You mean Sara?" she retorted, and then flushed, because she realized she was confusing what she had seen in the trailer with Sara, the pregnant sow back at home.

"No, not SARA. SIRI. S . . . I . . . R . . . I," Jacks enunciated each letter carefully.

"I have no idea what it means."

"Do you think the elephant ought to be destroyed?"

"No. But I also think it should be retired from any kind of performing with humans."

"I see. Well, thank you, Miss Nightingale," Jacks said. "I mean, Dr. Nightingale."

Didi left the tent, went back to the jeep and helped Charlie unload the supplies. They stored them in a large freestanding bin that also held rakes, shovels, and several other specialized tools that were used to service the many heaters and blowers that warmed the tents, trailers, and trucks during winter performances. The supplies that had to be refrigerated were put in the administrative trailer, which had a small but complete kitchen.

Charlie kept speculating about the suicide. "Loss of face," he kept saying. "The boy just lost too much face when his Dolly killed that girl." Didi felt she didn't know enough to affirm or deny his theory.

Then she saw that the elephants had been removed from the trailers and brought to the enclosure. She and Charlie walked over and peered through the chain link fence. It was obvious that the two remaining dancing girls had carried out the task. Now they were feeding and watering all five elephants, including the murderess, Dolly.

Didi formally introduced herself and Charlie to Linda Septiem and Gwyn Masters through the fence.

How pretty they are, even in their work clothes, Didi thought as she watched the two agile young women—about her own age or younger—fork bales of hay to the elephants. The big beasts proceeded joyously to break the bales apart with their trunks and eat. The space they were in began to steam from the interaction of warm bodies and cold air.

Didi wondered what these dancing girls thought about the death of Ti Nolan. How did they deal with the world of chance? It might just as well have been either of them who'd been pulverized by Dolly.

"Is that all they get—hay?" Charlie whispered in Didi's ear.

"No, this is obviously just a quickie feeding until the new handler arrives. They're supposed to get fruits and vegetables along with the fodder. In fact, Charlie, each elephant should get at least two hundred pounds a day in bulk food."

"That's a lot of apples," Charlie muttered, impressed.

"It's only half of what they eat in the wild, but then again . . . I don't know if there is such a thing as a wild Asian elephant anymore. Anyway, they should also get some kind of bran mash—to help their digestion. Elephants in the wild only digest half of what they devour. The other half passes right through the system."

"How can I be a dairy farmer and not have a soft spot in my heart for manure factories," said old Charlie nostalgically.

Didi laughed and was about to point out that he was not a dairy farmer anymore, that he hadn't been one for a long time; that he was now a veterinary technician. But at the last moment she held back. Charlie Gravis didn't have to be reminded of that sad fact. And he did consider it sad.

The five Asian elephants were now really getting into their feed. Didi watched, fascinated and charmed. She tried to pick them out by name—which was Queen and which Alma—which Lutzi and which Gorgeous. But the only one she could name for sure was Dolly. They were beginning to get playful, flinging the hay every which way and then spritzing water over one another's back. Like five tipsy matrons going to the baths together in Saratoga Springs.

"What do we do now?" Charlie asked, obviously growing weary of Didi's intense scrutiny of the beasts.

"Well, I have to stay on the grounds until the new handler shows up. Why don't you find someplace warm, Charlie, and take a nap."

He sauntered off. Didi watched the elephants for another half an hour, then walked to the ring where the Shelty Sisters were giving their ponies a workout in lieu of the usual matinee, which had once again been canceled, this time because of Tran's bloody suicide.

The little people were superb horsewomen. The secrets of the success of their act were gaits and leads—the ponies had to move in unison over an extended period of time without speeding up or slowing down, except when told to—and then they had to adjust quickly, or a Shelty would fall on her head. Didi studied the hardy ponies as they circled the ring. They appeared to be in top shape. She could tell by their coats, manes, and tails that they had been brushed earlier that morning, and were probably groomed every morning. There was not the slightest hint of lameness in any of them.

Didi then moved to the covered cage where Lothar Strauss was putting his big cats through their paces. It was an elaborately constructed portable contraption, heated by blowers because the big cats might have some trouble with cold weather. After all, they were *Bengals*, not *Siberians*. Elephants and ponies could handle any kind of weather. Heated, portable tents and cages, Didi realized, enabled a small circus to tour during "off" months—when other kinds of rural entertainment such as state and county fairs were scarce. Of course there was also the fact that February in Upstate New York is traditionally milder than December, January, or March. It was one of those anomalies of weather that no one could explain.

Didi stayed a long way from the action. She

didn't even enter the heated area because she knew that shadows could spook tigers. As she watched Lothar roughhousing with the cats, she felt her chest constrict. It wasn't fear but apprehension. She had never treated, much less examined, a Bengal tiger. The power of them! Their brilliant coats . . . the sheer speed and threat to their movements . . . it was all breathtaking. She found herself sinking into a kind of awe-filled Blakean well—decidedly unprofessional.

"Dr. Nightingale!"

She turned quickly toward the sound, jumped, as if she were a child caught red-handed at some shocking mischief.

Thomas Allenbach was approaching. "Pak Pavala has landed in Albany," he said, beaming, almost conspiratorial. "He should be here in about two hours." Then he veered off, took a quick look in at the cat cage, and walked on, a distinct bounce in his stride.

Didi made her way back to the administrative trailer, where she assumed Charlie had gone to rest his weary bones. She felt, as she walked, a growing excitement, as if something very good was about to happen. She laughed out loud and began to sing snatches of a song she had heard recently on one of those "golden oldies" radio stations— "Rock With Me, Baby."

But she stopped as quickly as she had begun, embarrassed at the inappropriateness of her sudden joy. It must be, she thought, a temporary intoxication from being so close to elephants and tigers. Oh my, no dairy cows, these.

Just as Didi reached for the trailer door latch she had a quick and bittersweet memory of her mother. How she would have loved being here with her daughter . . . making the rounds with her in a circus. How long had her mom been dead now—three years? Perhaps four. Didi had lost track, but she missed her more now than during that first year of grief.

She opened the door and saw Charlie sleeping soundly in the swivel chair. She felt a sudden enormous affection for the difficult old coot. She remembered telling him once, after his failure to follow her instructions had gotten him a swift kick from an ornery horse, that "the chickens had come home to roost." Charlie had taken the pain stoically and replied: "But whose chickens are they?" Good old Charlie Gravis, former dairy man.

Chapter 6

Allie Voegler heard the news report on the circus suicide as he was driving toward the Hillsbrook Arboretum, where Officer Storch had found several objects that had probably been taken in the Dunlop break-in.

The radio report also mentioned the death a day earlier of the circus dancer. The young girl, the announcer explained matter-of-factly, had been crushed to death by the performing elephant she had been riding.

Had Didi heard about all this? Allie wondered. He knew how she loved circuses. He looked at the clock on the dashboard. Didi would be in her small animal clinic just about now, and her place was a short drive away—no more than a ten-minute detour.

Allie made an on-the-spot decision and swerved off the main road. As he drove he flicked the radio dial from station to station, trying to get more news of the circus troubles, but there was none.

Eight minutes later he pulled up in front of Dr. Nightingale's clinic. It was closed, the blinds drawn, all the lights out. Allie groaned, climbed out of his car and walked around to the back of the house, followed by at least a half-dozen sniffing dogs and as many tiptoeing cats, all of whom seemed to materialize out of thin air.

Before he could knock at the kitchen door, it opened. There stood Mrs. Tunney, clad in several sweaters with a tatty housecoat over all. Allie looked past her and saw Abigail seated at the long kitchen table. She was handling an enormous pile of root vegetables, cakey earth still clinging to their tops.

"Can I help you, Officer Voegler?" Mrs. Tunney asked.

Allie smiled. This woman, he knew, had never liked him—not since he was a kid delivering groceries to Didi's mother. Well, he didn't think too much of her either. In fact, that went for old Tunney and the whole crew of sponging eccentrics who now had attached themselves to Didi as they had to her mother. He particularly didn't like the bizarre role they had played in secretly warehousing stolen falcon chicks on Didi's property—a fact that had emerged during the investigation into the murder of dairy farmer Dick Obey. But Didi had defended them, forgiven them. For a moment Allie looked away from the kitchen, toward the massive pine stand that began not more than two hundred yards from the house, across a now dormant alfalfa field. He remembered walking in there with Didi . . . he remembered. Then he turned back to Mrs. Tunney.

"I see the clinic's closed this afternoon," he noted.

"No, it isn't."

He could tell it was going to be like pulling teeth.

"I came to see Didi."

"Oh? To see Miss Quinn?"

"To see Didi Nightingale. Is she around?"

"No."

"Would you tell me where she is . . . please."

"Miss Quinn is away on business," Mrs. Tunney said regally.

"Look here, Mrs. Tunney—"

"At the circus, of course," she interrupted, smiling insincerely, "where she is the official veterinary consultant. Or didn't you know that, Officer?" With that, the door shut firmly in Allie's face.

Damnit, Allie thought, Didi always manages to be in the right place at the right time . . . or was it the right place at the wrong time?

He strode back to the car and drove quickly to the entrance gate of the arboretum. One of the town's most important tourist attractions, it was a wonderland of both imported and domestic trees, many of them quite rare. People from all over the world journeyed to the arboretum in all seasons, not a few scientists among them.

Officer Storch was waiting impatiently for him. A tall, attractive woman in her fifties waited alongside him. She had white hair cut very short and she was woefully underdressed for the weather, wearing only what seemed to be an ancient riding jacket over her dress.

"This is May Dunlop," Officer Storch said. Mrs. Dunlop offered Allie her hand. In the other hand she held a crumpled piece of paper.

Then Storch headed off onto the rocky trail that circled the arboretum. It was an easy path to follow; the fence that separated the arboretum from the main road was always on the left and the trees always on the right. The problem was the tricky footing on the icy and sometimes slushy trail. Storch and Allie slipped and stumbled again and again, but Mrs. Dunlop's steps were sure and effortless.

Allie began to recall the village gossip about Mrs. Charles Dunlop: that she had once been a great horsewoman; that she was older than her husband and had been promiscuous in her younger days; that she had been a patient in a mental hospital downstate; that she was now an alcoholic. Of all the rumors, the only one Allie believed was that she had been a good horsewoman—she still had that balance.

Suddenly Officer Storch called out: "Take a look!"

Just where the trail dipped in and out of a small ravine and the fence between road and trail was lower, someone had flung what appeared to be garbage over the fence.

But it wasn't really garbage, and a lot that was thrown didn't clear the fence; it had fallen back onto the shoulder of the road or got caught in the barbed wire on top of the fence.

"Yes," May Dunlop said calmly, "it's all from our house."

She then held up the crushed paper she'd been holding, as if confirming her statement. Allie realized it must be a list of what had been stolen.

He could see on the ground knives and forks and clocks and necklaces and brooches and small objets d'art that had been wrapped in tablecloths and towels that had unrolled when flung.

Officer Storch analyzed the situation. "The way I see it, Allie, the kids sobered up and tried to sell the stuff. They couldn't move it, though, because they didn't know where to go, so they just dumped everything."

He paused for a moment, turning over in his hand a silver serving spoon he had picked up. "Or it could be," he added, "that they never tried to fence the stuff at all. Maybe when they came to their senses they realized how much trouble they could get into and just ditched everything, too scared or ashamed to bring it back to the Dun-lops'."

Allie nodded. The scenarios that Storch had laid out made sense. Both of them. Apparently May Dunlop agreed, because she, too, was nod-ding.

The three of them headed back slowly. But just ten seconds into their retreat, May stopped and pointed with one gloved hand to the far side of the trail.

"Over there! Can you see them?"

"Oh my God!" Storch cried, already storming off. "There they are—the fishing rods!"

He reached the spot and picked up five or six slender jagged pieces of wood. "Goddamnit, why did those stupid kids have to go and do that? No cause to break them apart like that."

Allie recalled Storch's awestruck handling of the remaining antique fly rods at the Dunlops'. He felt sorry for Storch, as if the loss had been his rather than Charles Dunlop's. He looked over at May Dunlop then, and was startled to see that she was smiling.

Mrs. Dunlop was also speaking, but it was a low mumble that Allie could not hear. "Excuse me?" he said.

She turned to him full face, and he could see that the smile was less than joyous.

"I was saying that few people understand how deep the cruelty can run in Dutchess County."

Allie didn't know what to say. He didn't know

what the hell she was talking about. Somehow he didn't think it was the destroyed antiques. But he did know that, standing in the dirty snow, she was the epitome of a beautiful, strong, and wise horse-woman.

Chapter 7

A face appeared. A very strange face. A woman's face dotted with beads of sweat. Then the face grinned. The grin became a wound. The wound dripped blood.

Didi woke from her nap in terror. She realized that the face in the dream had been that of the dancing girl—but the wounds had been Tran Van Minh's.

It was dark. Where was she?

She heard Charlie Gravis's voice from a distance. She remembered entering the trailer and finding Charlie asleep. She must have fallen off also. She scrambled to her feet and opened the door. Charlie was standing outside, alternately chewing on an unlit cigar and singing "Annie Laurie"—about the limit of his repertoire. Didi looked at her watch, the hands clearly visible now that the sun had gone down and the outside lighting of the circus grounds turned on. It was only 5:00 P.M. But the sun had totally vanished. February.

"Hope you had a good nap, Miss Quinn," Charlie said good-naturedly, "because here comes trouble." He gestured with his cigar toward the two approaching figures.

For a moment, Didi's anger flared. Why did they always call her Miss Quinn, Charlie and the others at home? Why not Miss Nightingale if they were going to address her formally? Why always with her mother's maiden name? She had had a father and his name was Nightingale. Of course he was dead a long time and their allegiance had been to her mother; it was her mother who had taken them in like lost sheep. Didi caught hold of herself. This was not the time for a useless remonstrance with her geriatric and very stubborn veterinary assistant.

Walking toward them were Thomas Allenbach and a small, sturdily built man.

Allenbach introduced them. "Dr. Didi Quinn Nightingale, I would like you to meet Pak Pavala."

The little brown man bowed and took Didi's proffered hand in a firm grip. Then he released it. He was no taller than Tran had been, but he was much broader, especially in the face. He wore a bright red wool Mackinaw and a black beret. Didi noticed he carried a long clay pipe like those she had seen during her graduate project in the Southeast Asian logging camps. At night, when the elephants were tethered, the handlers would sit around the fire and smoke the pipes.

"Do you speak English?" Didi asked.

"A little. Very little," the elephant handler answered, almost blushing.

"Pak is going to put them to bed," Allenbach said. Pak nodded and walked off. Didi followed him according to the prearranged plan. Allenbach and Charlie stayed where they were.

First Pak inspected the three big elephant trailers. They were obviously converted horse trailers—the ones that mounted police used to transport six horses at a time. Each trailer had been stripped down and converted to handle two elephants and each was spotlessly clean. There was hay and water and tubs of either fruit or potatoes in each. Didi noticed that the sides of the reconverted trailers were floridly painted with the figures of white elephants costumed in silk halters and jeweled diadems. She realized that these were the same kinds of paintings that used to appear on the national flags of Siam, before it became Thailand. She remembered that during that first tragic matinee she had attended, vendors in the ring apron were selling small satiny flags with the same emblem on them. Well, what child would not like a small flag with a white elephant on it? Little did the children know, Didi reflected, that up until the 19th century whole kingdoms went to war over the possession of albino elephants, which were supposed to be reincarnations of the Buddha.

Pak nodded to her that everything was fine after he finished his inspection of the trailers. Then they both walked to the elephant enclosure where the beasts were tethered. Pak motioned that he wanted to go in alone at first, so Didi hung back. She watched him carefully.

He sauntered in, singing some unidentifiable ditty, very low, but audible. The floodlights around the enclosure illuminated him to the elephants and they watched him warily. He walked up and down the line, in and out, unconcerned, as if he was not interested in their well-being at all. Then he started a second tour, and this time, Didi saw, he made some bodily contact with each elephant, on each side—touching legs and trunks and bellies. Always, always, keeping up that monotonous singsong. Didi watched with increasing fascination; he was a master.

On his third circle of the beasts, he tapped each one on the shoulder with the clay pipe and at the same time gave each one a small piece of rock salt. The elephants consumed it greedily and happily.

Pak Pavala calmly untethered each elephant and led her to her trailer. The elephants followed him docilely, unquestioningly, as if they'd known him for years. It was an astonishing performance and Didi felt like applauding when the handler had finished the task. But he seemed to be utterly unself-conscious of his skills. All he said to Didi was, "I will sleep now. In same place with Gorgeous." Then he shook her hand, and walked off.

Didi marched back to the administrative trailer. Charlie was still outside, this time smoking his cigar in earnest. "It's time to go home, Charlie."

"You said a mouthful, Miss Quinn," he replied and flicked the cold ashes of his cigar.

It was a long ride home. Didi was so tired she could barely keep her eyes open, but she just didn't trust Charlie behind the wheel. To the old man's consternation, she put on tape after tape of Patsy Cline, playing the music at ear-shattering volume.

When they finally reached the house, Didi quickly checked the log and the answering machine in the small animal clinic. There had been a few calls and a few referrals. Nothing major. Her staff had done their job well. Then she went upstairs to her room—to what had been her mother's room—lay down thankfully, and fell fast asleep in an instant.

The phone woke her on its fifth ring. She groped about for it in a stupor.

"Dr. Nightingale! It's Tom!"

She had no idea who Tom was. Didi looked over at the clock radio. Good god, it was four-thirty in the morning! *Who was Tom?*

She was swinging her feet over the side of the bed, preparatory to screaming at the fool who had awakened her from a deep and deserved sleep, when suddenly she realized who was on the other end of the line.

"Mr. Allenbach?"

"Yes, it's me. I'm sorry to wake you at this crazy hour. But one of our elephants is sick. It's Gorgeous. You better get here."

"As soon as I can."

She dressed quickly, left a note for Charlie in the kitchen, ran out of the house, cursed the jeep when it took too long to fire up, and then headed for the circus grounds.

As she screamed into the parking lot she felt the excitement flowing in her veins. Sure, she was angry at being roused from her sleep at this ungodly hour, but when all was said and done, this sort of thing was what she was all about—it was why she had become a vet. She was only doing what she had been trained to do, with creatures she loved.

Tom Allenbach emerged out of the darkness, speaking just as rapidly as he was walking toward Didi. Pak Pavala hadn't wanted him to disturb Didi, he said; Pak believed he could handle the situation himself. "But look, Dr. Nightingale, we can't afford any more problems."

Didi started to tell him about Southeastern Asian elephant trainers, how they would as soon keep their money in a bank as depend on a western-trained veterinarian. They used an ancient handbook that prescribed specific remedies for ailments of elephants—wounds were to be treated with butter salves, inflammations with warm, bloody deer meat, and so on. But Allenbach had hold of Didi's elbow and was rushing her along, and they were at the elephant trailer before she could finish explaining.

Pak stepped out to greet them. Didi peered inside. The other elephant had been removed. Gorgeous was in there alone. She was quiet, very quiet.

Didi motioned that Allenbach should stay where he was. To Pak she made a different gesture, asking him to lead the way inside.

She studied Gorgeous for a few moments from a distance, then moved closer.

Yes, there was no doubt of it; the elephant was ill.

First of all, Gorgeous was actually slumped against the side of the trailer. Her big ears were pulled back, folded against her shoulders and neck. She didn't flap them once. And her usually active tail hung limply down.

Didi calmly reached out and began to touch Gorgeous's trunk in several places, then ran her hand the length of the animal's foreleg and along the body.

Gorgeous was warm to the touch. Fever. Not a high one, but fever nonetheless.

Didi walked about three feet away from the elephant and stood next to Pak. She was almost certain what the trouble was—a streptococcus infection. Not uncommon in zoo elephants.

She knew what had to be done. Old-fashioned sulfonamide therapy in powdered form—about four hundred grams. Just mix it into her water. If that didn't work—and sometimes elephants are very taste-sensitive even when ill—there was always penicillin. Just find a soft spot under the foreleg and inject it. Didi mentally calculated the dosage. It was staggering. About fifteen-thousand units for an animal that size.

But first she had to confirm the diagnosis. She turned to Pak. "Is she eating?"

"Won't eat. Eat nothing."

Eating nothing. Well, that fell right into the profile. Didi nodded happily.

"And she can't get enough water—right?"

Pak looked at her dumbly for a moment, then said: "No. No water. Nothing."

Didi thought the language difficulty had confused him. "She wants water all the time. Isn't that right, Pak?"

"No! No water. Eat nothing. Drink nothing."

Didi stood dumbfounded. Her diagnosis had collapsed. Elephants with streptococcus infection were always thirsty. Her confidence deflated as quickly as her diagnosis. For the first time she realized her own arrogance at taking this job regardless of the money. She really didn't know much about the big beasts. Not much at all. Maybe, she thought, Allenbach had just made up the story that she had been highly recommended to him. Maybe he just needed any old vet to work for that kind of money . . . just to have a vet on the premises to protect the circus legally.

She needed help and she needed it fast. Didi walked out of the trailer and said to a waiting Allenbach: "I'm going to have to make some calls." She went to the administrative trailer and dialed her old professor from veterinary school at Penn—Hiram Bechtold. It was only after she heard his dazed voice on the other end of the line that she remembered it was five-thirty in the morning.

She apologized profusely and Bechtold took it in good humor. She told him the problem. He couldn't help. But he knew someone who could: an old friend who had been a vet at the Cincinnati Zoo before he retired. His name was Jefferson Smith and he now raised bird dogs in South Carolina. Bechtold gave Didi the number.

Heedless of the hour, she put in the call to Dr. Smith. The phone rang and rang but there was no answer. She hung up. A minute later she dialed the number again. Again no answer. She ripped off her wristwatch, laid it on the phone stand, and began to time five-minute intervals. At the end of every interval she called the number again. Her professional cool was dissolving rapidly. There had been so much tragedy in this circus already; the idea of Gorgeous dying was intolerable. Particularly if it was because of a young vet's diagnostic inexperience or ineptitude.

On the twelfth try, a kindly southern voice answered. Didi introduced herself and told Jefferson Smith that Hiram had given her his number. After several moments of strained chat about dear old Hiram, Didi laid out—concisely and thoroughly—what she'd found in her quick examination of the elephant.

There was a long pause as the retired vet more than a thousand miles away digested the information.

"Where is the old girl being kept?"

"In a converted horse trailer."

"A lot of feed around?"

"Yes."

"Hay?"

"Bales of it."

There was another long pause and then Jefferson Smith said, "Well, Dr. Nightingale, I would do nothing."

"Nothing!"

"Nothing. It may just be something she picked up from the feed. Maybe a parasite. Or maybe a reaction to pesticides. A lot of elephants have the very devil with pesticides."

"You mean in the hay?"

"Sure."

Didi heard furious barking in the background. Jefferson Smith laughed indulgently. "They're just a little excited today," he commented, and then said: "Take her out of the trailer. Bring her into a clean space. Under a tent is fine. Just tether her, leave her a tub of water and some nice succulent heads of lettuce, and watch her.

"That's all?"

"That's it."

Didi thanked him profusely and hung up. She would do exactly as he suggested. Did she have an option? When she left the trailer it was morning and light. The roustabouts set up a separate tent. The ground was swept clean. Gorgeous was brought inside and tethered. Vats of water and vegetables were left within easy reach. Then Didi began the ritual of waiting.

She decided to spend the entire twenty-four-hour period with the elephant. It was the least she could do. Pak kept her company much of the time, but in the afternoon his services were required in the big ring. The matinee went on as scheduled even though only three of the five elephants could appear. Poor Dolly was of course still quarantined. Charlie showed up that afternoon, having been driven from Hillsbrook by Trent Tucker in his ramshackle truck. He was toting a huge paper sack filled with sandwiches for Didi, along with a few of Mrs. Tunney's deviled eggs.

When it was dark, Pak set up heaters and a small cot for Didi. She would sleep under the tent with her patient. Pak slept, as usual, in one of the elephant vans. Charlie decided to stay on the grounds, too, so he slept in the administrative trailer.

The night passed slowly. Twelve hours went by . . . then fifteen . . . sixteen. By the light of a small battery lamp Didi read a book of short stories by Saki. Allenbach had given it to her. When she was tired of reading she paced. When she grew tired of pacing she did her breathing exercises. Always she kept an eye on Gorgeous. But there was no observable change at all in the elephant. She had the same low grade fever; she was still listless; she still refused to eat or drink.

It was after one in the morning when Didi finally fell asleep—fully clothed—on her folding cot.

It was just after six in the morning when a stream of water sloshed across her face and woke her with such a shock that the cot was overturned in the process. She scrambled to her feet, trying at the same time to spit out the sudden avalanche of water.

Then she looked up into the huge face of grinning Gorgeous. Yes, Gorgeous had spritzed her with the water and now she was calmly selecting choice heads of lettuce from one of the tubs, picking each one up daintily with her trunk and transporting it to her mouth, and there grinding the delicacy to bits with her powerful molars.

Gorgeous seemed one hundred percent recovered. Her ears were flaring to beat the band; her tail was twitching happily; and there was a gleam of mischief in her eye. What's more, she had no fever at all. Didi was about to call Pak, but the commotion had already wakened him and he was right there beside her, looking on happily and sucking on his clay pipe. An hour later, a very happy Didi and Charlie Gravis were heading back to Hillsbrook in the red jeep.

The cause for celebration did not end with the trip home. Fat Sara the pig had finally given birth and there were eight in the litter. Abigail had virtually taken up residence in the farrowing pen with the tiny piglets to make sure they were warm, well fed, and not crushed by their mother.

Didi felt so good in fact that she decided to take the rest of the day off and go shopping. She cajoled Mrs. Tunney into accompanying her to the Fishkill Mall, where Didi purchased five paperbacks, two tins of imported tea, a pound of Kenyan coffee, two sweatshirts, spiffy new hiking sneakers, and a pair of earrings in the shape of pandas made in the People's Republic of China. For Mrs. Tunney, she bought one oversized towel and a shower cap.

By the time they arrived back home it was late afternoon. Didi decided to take all her elves out to dinner at the Hillsbrook Diner. All except Abigail, that is, who remained with Sara and her newborns. Didi noticed that all her retainers at one time or another during the meal were secreting scraps of every conceivable kind—no doubt for the triumphant sow.

It had been a glorious day, Didi mused as she drove her charges back. A sick elephant recovered . . . Sara's adorable litter . . . a successful shopping trip . . . a communal dinner eaten with gusto and without strife.

The entire household went to sleep early that night and Trent Tucker seemed able to get the furnace to really hum. The large stone farmhouse with its many ill-conceived additions was actually toasty.

In the morning, Didi awoke as usual at six o'clock. She dressed and walked down the stairs, through the hallway, and into the large kitchen to make a quick cup of coffee before going outside to perform her yogic breathing ritual.

But this morning, waiting for her in a row at the kitchen table was the entire compliment of elves—a most unusual occurrence.

She looked questioningly at each of them before addressing her "Yes . . . ?" to the group.

Mrs. Tunney tried to stifle her laugh but couldn't.

Charlie Gravis wordlessly turned the pages of the morning edition of the *Dutchess County Daily Star* and held the opened newspaper across his chest.

Didi found herself looking at a photograph of . . . herself. She was seated on an iron cot keeping a worried vigil over Gorgeous the elephant. Next to that was another photo of her with her hand on Gorgeous's wrinkled trunk.

Over the pictures ran a bold headline: LADY VET FROM HILLSBROOK SAVES HER TWO-TON CLIENT.

Didi sat down in a kind of shock. Who could possibly have taken those pictures? She hadn't seen a soul anywhere near the tent. She took the paper from Charlie and read the accompanying story.

A brilliant young veterinarian from Hillsbrook, it said, a graduate of the prestigious University of Pennsylvania, who had returned home to practice in her native dairy cow country, had turned the tide of bad luck for a visiting circus by saving one of its most precious assets—the elephant called, rightly, Gorgeous.

"You're famous," Charlie declared.

"We're all famous," Trent Tucker added.

"And I'm also very embarrassed," Didi said.

"Maybe," Mrs. Tunney mused, "they'll put you on TV. Maybe you'll become a TV star on one of those talk shows, or *Live at Five* or something— and then we can all get rich."

Didi stared at the photographs. The shots of her were none too flattering. But Gorgeous had turned out to be extremely photogenic. She looked like the mother of all elephants.

"Oh, damn!" she suddenly exclaimed, startling all the elves. "I forgot to call Jefferson Smith," she said, and ran into the office to dial the South Carolina number. The retired veterinarian turned dog breeder accepted her thanks graciously. He invited her down there any time she wanted to come, alone or accompanying Hiram Bechtold.

Didi sat for a moment at her desk after making the call. She realized that there was one other thing she had to do: find the source of the contaminated feed that had made Gorgeous sick.

Chapter 8

"What are you looking for?" Charlie asked.

"Contamination. Infestation. Blight. Rust. You name it, Charlie. If you see anything let me know. Why don't you start with those hay bales over there."

Charlie nodded and walked slowly to the hay. Didi began to open one dumpster at a time. The bins held food for the circus animals and because it was winter they functioned as natural and inexpensive refrigeration units.

"It could be a parasite, Charlie . . . or a fungus. You just have to keep your eyes open. Be on the lookout for any change or discoloration."

"I always keep my eyes open, Miss Quinn," he retorted with a hurt inflection. He pulled some hay from one of the bales and broke the straws between his palms. Then he buried his nose in his cupped hands and inhaled deeply. Charlie rubbed the straws again and took another long whiff. Then he put one between his lips and chewed it, as dairy farmers have always done. "It's just good Timothy hay," he pronounced.

Didi looked at him severely and pointed to the many other blocks that had to be tested—however he wanted to test them. But one sampling was not enough.

She opened one dumpster after another, checking the contents. There were fruits, vegetables, and meat for the big cats and carrots for the Shetlands. Finding the contaminant, Didi realized, was going to be a difficult quest, because it could be just about anything . . . perhaps locoweed or milk vetch or hound's tooth or any other common weed that might be toxic. And, of course, it could be a pesticide, many of the more deadly ones being totally odorless.

She came to the dumpster that contained the bran mash supplement. There were two large cardboard vats of the pellets. Using the scoop that lay on the top of each vat, Didi carefully sifted through all the pellets. This kind of supplement was particularly susceptible to egg-laying flies. It was exhausting work and her arms soon began to ache. She kept switching the scoop from right hand to left hand and then back again. No, she realized, the contamination wasn't here; the vats were clean.

As she was closing the top of the dumpster she spotted two discarded cardboard containers that had been crushed and folded. Didi pulled them out and dragged them toward the garbage heap.

Halfway there, she stopped. A strangely pungent odor was emanating from the cardboard. She dropped the containers onto the ground and knelt beside them. The scent was peculiar, indeed. And yet she seemed to recognize it. She knew somehow that she recognized it, but she was unable really to place it, give it a name.

"Charlie, come over here a minute, would you?"

He walked over gamely.

"There was bran mash in these vats. Can you smell anything else on that cardboard?"

Charlie sniffed audibly. Then he broke into a smile.

"What is it, Charlie? What's so funny?"

"That smell brings back memories, Miss Quinn . . . memories of Iwo."

"Iwo? What does that mean?"

"Iwo Jima, Miss Quinn. It's an island in the Pacific."

Didi felt like an idiot. Of course she knew where Iwo Jima was. And of course she'd known that Charlie had served in the Pacific in World War II. But what did that have to do with anything?

"You know," he said gently, "me and Calvin Rackstraw—another fella from Hillsbrook—we enlisted together in the Marines. And all through boot camp and the trip over and the first islands, Calvin and me were never separated. Then, the minute we hit Iwo, they transfer him. I don't see him for a few days, and the next time I do see him . . . he's dead. Coming down the hill on a stretcher. Deader than—" Charlie stopped talking, obviously choked up.

She did not know what to do. Charlie's memories seemed to be getting out of hand. She wanted to lead the conversation back to the weird odor of the cardboard containers. But it would be rude, and useless, to try to interrupt him now. He'd get back to the point in his own good time, by his own route.

"The night after Calvin died, they were coming at us with everything. Mortars, banzai attacks, everything. We stopped them right at the trench line. One of their dead tumbled into our trench. He was shot all to pieces. He was like Swiss cheese. But the funniest thing was that he had all these little bottles tied onto his belt . . . like grenades . . . and with all that shooting, not one of those bottles got broke." He halted his story again while he fished a cigar out of his shirt pocket.

"Know what was in those bottles, Miss Quinn?"

"No, Charlie, I don't."

"Sake."

"Oh? Well, that's . . . interesting."

"You bet it's interesting, Miss Quinn. That rice wine was sweet and strong. Good stuff."

Charlie pointed down at the flattened cardboard. "That's what you're smelling there."

"Sake?"

"Yessir."

"Charlie, are you sure?"

"I am, Miss Quinn. I'll never forget that smell."

Didi suddenly covered her face with her hands.

"What is it, Miss Quinn?"

She did not reply. Nor did she remove her hands from her face immediately. But she did nod that she was all right.

When Didi finally pulled her hands away she was pale. "Charlie," she said, "your war story may have answered a very important question. Tell me, have you ever heard of arrack?"

"No. Is it an island . . . like Iwo?"

"No, it's a rice wine . . . like sake. And it has been around a long, long time. People who like to read about elephants always run into that word. Do you know why, Charlie?"

"Miss Quinn, maybe you should sit down for a minute."

"I'm fine, Charlie. Just fine. But this wine, arrack . . . You see, around the first and second centuries, elephants were the most important attack units in the armies. But there was a problem with them. First, you needed to be very persuasive to make them charge during battle. Elephants tend to charge only when they're good and ready to. Second, and more important, elephants are kind and gentle animals. They really don't like to maim or kill living things. So they were given arrack. It seems that alcohol had the same effect on the elephants that it has on some humans: it made them violent."

"Well, that's a nice piece of information, Miss Quinn. Can't say I ever heard that before."

Didi's face clouded over. "Don't you see why I told you that story, Charlie? Don't you understand what I'm saying?"

Charlie didn't answer.

"It was murder, Charlie."

"What was?"

"The death of Ti Nolan."

"That girl who danced on the elephant?"

"Yes, yes, the dancing girl. If someone put sake in Dolly's bran mash before the matinee, it was bloody well murder."

"Oh, miss, I don't see how you're coming to that conclusion."

Didi wasn't listening. She was deep in thought now. This was an incredible turn of events. It was difficult to believe. But it was there . . . in one's face. The bran mash was saturated with sake. But was it given to all the elephants? Obviously not. Well, perhaps not so obviously. Maybe not. Maybe only Dolly got the sake-laced mash and the other elephants got the normal feed. Did the madman who did this want to kill all the dancers? Or only Ti Nolan?

Everything about this circus, these people, these animals, was becoming crazier and more unbelievable, and more lethal.

Didi shook her head vigorously, as if clearing out spider webs. She picked up the cardboard and sniffed it again.

"Do me a favor, Charlie. Smell this again."

"Surely. Whatever you want, Miss Quinn." He took the crushed cartons from her almost reverentially. When he had inhaled deeply, he pronounced, "This is sake. I swear it is."

Now what? Didi thought. What do I do now? She thought of that state trooper who had questioned everyone after Tran Van Minh's suicide. What was his name? Jacks. Yes. She could go to him with this. But then she thought better of it. No, not to him. To Allie Voegler. Even though this was outside his jurisdiction. It had to be Allie. He was a friend as well as a cop. He would listen.

"Charlie, we're taking a spin back to Hillsbrook," she said.

"Fine with me," he replied, and the two of them climbed into the jeep, stowing the crushed cartons on the floor.

Didi drove very slowly, so slowly that Charlie begged her to let him take over. He was so solicitous of her welfare that he actually suggested she play some of her Patsy Cline tapes. But she demurred. She was fine, she said. She was just turning over in her mind all the possible explanations that *didn't* add up to murder: Maybe the handler had been careless, or drunk, and somehow his supply of sake had wound up in the elephant's feed? Maybe someone else at the circus—a sort of big-top version of Charlie Gravis—considered rice wine a fine old herbal tonic for pachyderms and had given the elephant a liberal dose of it? No, no.

It was inconceivable that anyone with any knowledge of elephants would ever knowingly give alcohol to one of the beasts. It was a recipe for disaster. It was a recipe for murder. Had Tran done it? Was that why he killed himself?

"Miss Quinn! You missed the turnoff," Charlie said accusingly.

"We're not going home just yet," Didi said. "We're going into town."

"Do some shopping, huh?"

"No. To find Allie Voegler."

And she did find him—lounging, predictably, by the coffee machine in the temporary hut that housed the Hillsbrook Police Department while their fancy new quarters were being constructed.

"Well, look who's here. I've been trying to catch up with you for two days. I thought you'd pulled some kind of disappearing act. And then Mrs. Tunney tells me you went and joined the circus. In fact, you're a circus hero. I saw your picture in the paper."

"Was it a good one?" she asked coyly.

"Nothing could look as good as you in person," Allie replied.

Didi took in the compliment but said nothing in return. Since she had moved back to Hillsbrook to practice, Allie Voegler had been the closest thing to a romantic interest in her life. The affection was there between them, and the promise was there, and they sought each other's company often. The attraction was strong. But there was tension between them when they were together, and fights. There was an undeniable chemistry, but it was not really the kind of romance she wanted. When all was said and done, there was just something about Allie she didn't fully trust. So they had not become lovers.

Of course, Allie believed it was because she was a social climber . . . that she wanted a different kind of man. The kind of man on his way up in the world.

Whatever the reason, they had never been lovers.

"How's it going at the circus, Didi?" he asked.

"You heard about the dancing girl and the suicide?"

"Sure."

"It's getting worse, Allie."

"How could that be?"

"Do me a favor and come outside with me for a minute. I want to show you something in the jeep."

"Okay."

Charlie had wandered off on some mission. Didi opened the car door and pulled out one of the crushed cartons.

"This," she said, "is a carton that used to contain bran mash supplements for the circus elephants. Look at the discolored and damp edges, Allie. Someone obviously soaked the bran mash pellets in something. Now just smell the edges."

He leaned forward and sniffed. "Alcohol," he muttered.

"Sake, to be specific."

"So?"

"It is highly dangerous to give an elephant alcohol before it performs with a live human on its back, Allie."

"Why is that?"

"Like humans, they can get very mean under the influence."

"You're going somewhere, but I really don't know where, Didi."

"The dancing girl was murdered, Officer Voegler. That's where I'm going."

"Whoa! Take it easy. How do you get from alcohol on a piece of cardboard to murder?"

"It's easy . . . I think."

"Well, Madame Vet," he said, "some would call that thinking and some would call it something else."

Didi grabbed the cardboard out of his hands, thrust it back into the jeep and slammed the door shut.

"Do you have anything else?" he asked, trying to salvage the meeting.

"What else do you need?"

"Motive, for example. Or a logical scenario of events. When was the alcohol put in the bran, or whatever it was? When was that particular batch given to this particular elephant? You know, stuff like that, Didi. Basic stuff."

"But those are the things I want you to find out. I want you to investigate."

"It's not my jurisdiction. The circus is not in the incorporated village of Hillsbrook. Or weren't you aware of that?"

"Allie," she said sadly, "she was a beautiful young woman."

"A lot of beautiful young people die, Didi. But if they don't die in Hillsbrook, I can't deal with it."

"A veterinarian doesn't worry about jurisdiction when an animal is sick."

"Damnit! I'm not a vet. I'm a police officer. I don't deal with cows—or elephants. I deal with people and laws. Get your damn priorities straight, will you?" In a fury he wheeled and walked back into the hut.

Didi shook her head grimly. She had been counting on help from him and there would apparently be none.

Charlie Gravis ambled back to the jeep then. He was carrying a waxed paper bag, holding it out as if it were an offering of some sort. "Late breakfast for you and me," he said.

They settled into the jeep and proceeded to wolf down the still-warm donuts he had bought.

"Are we going home now?" Charlie asked hopefully, balancing a paper cup of hot coffee on his knee.

"No, Charlie, I'm afraid not. We've got to go back to the circus again, to speak to Tom Allenbach."

"I take it that Officer Voegler didn't think much of your theory, Miss Quinn."

"You are absolutely correct, Mr. Gravis."

"Ah, you know these young fellas. Don't take it personally, Miss Quinn."

She started the engine. "I take it very personally, Charlie. I take everything personally. That's why I'm a veterinarian."

The little trailer was crowded. There was Allenbach, the circus manager, and Alfred Faulkner, the music man, and Laz Runay, the fire eater. They had all been there when Didi and Charlie arrived and she had made no effort to take Allenbach aside to tell him her story in private. The more the merrier, she figured.

Still, she addressed her words directly to Allenbach. When she had finished relating the story of the alcohol-soaked cartons, she ended with the statement: "So you can understand why I think that Ti Nolan was murdered."

The room was utterly silent. Allenbach looked extremely distressed and for a moment he stared wildly at his two companions.

"It's a terrible thing," Alfred Faulkner almost whispered. "If what you say is true, it's a terrible thing." He was not a young man, and running to fat, but his black hair was still very thick and it stood straight up.

"It's a lot more than terrible," Runay added indignantly. "Whoever did it ought to be hung."

"I have always thought," Allenbach lashed out, "that it was an old wives' tale, this thing about alcohol and elephants. About on a par with the belief that your warts will go away if you rub them with a potato and then feed the potato to a cow."

"Well," said Didi, a bit wryly, "the last large-scale use of elephants in wartime, as an attack force, occurred in the late fifteen century—in northern India—and the elephants were given *arrack* to bring out their ferocity. Believe me, under certain conditions, alcohol will make an elephant do very strange things."

There was another long silence. Finally Allenbach said, "Look, Dr. Nightingale, even if things happened the way you said, what do you expect me to do? And why didn't you go to the police? There seem to be state troopers here every day for one reason or another."

"All I want you to do is, first, confirm that what I say makes sense. Then we can figure out what to do and who to go to."

"Well, Doctor, you may have convinced my two gullible friends here"—and at this point the circus manager pointed a bit contemptuously at Faulkner and Runay—"but you haven't convinced me. In fact, I think you're making no sense at all."

The circus manager stood and walked around the small desk until he was no more than six inches away from Didi. There was in fact something so threatening in his manner that Charlie Gravis moved in protectively close to his boss.

Allenbach went on in a level voice. "I am not denying that there was liquor soaked into that container—maybe you're even right about it being sake. But it could have gotten there by sheer accident. And even if it didn't, anybody could have put it there. We use a lot of roustabouts. We pay them on a per day basis. In cash. Half of them are winos. It might have been any one of them."

He turned back to Faulkner and demanded: "Am I right, Alfred? Do I have a point or not?"

Faulkner nodded reluctantly. Laz Runay did not comment further.

Allenbach turned back to Didi, but this time his manner was warm, almost patronizing, as if she were a little child who needed instruction. "Let me explain what happened. We are simply having a streak of bad luck . . . very bad luck. That happens in circuses. It happens on Broadway. It happens to all groups of performers everywhere. Listen to me, Dr. Nightingale. Before we set up here we played Jamestown, New York. And before that, near Scranton. And before that we were just outside Harrisburg, Pennsylvania. The shows were all sold out. Everything went beautifully. The people loved us. There was not a single accident. Nothing went wrong. Everything was gold. You hear me? Then we come here—and boom! The ceiling caves in. Poor Ti gets crushed to death by one of the sweetest animals who ever lived. Tran, a gentle, devout man, slits his throat. Every day new kinds of officials are making inspections, hoping they can close us down. Everything has gone wrong. But that's just . . . show biz. We just have to ride it out without getting paranoid . . . without thinking that all kinds of evil forces are at work. It's just bad luck. And our luck will change again."

It was a long speech and Allenbach was exhausted by it, but it seemed finally to have convinced the sword swallower, who was nodding his head vigorously and looked almost ready to burst into applause. Allenbach walked to the small refrigerator, took out a bottle of apple juice, and offered it around. Only Charlie Gravis accepted some, in a paper cup pulled from a wall dispenser.

Allenbach replaced the juice in the refrigerator, sat back at his small desk, folded his arms, and waited for Didi to speak. She realized that it was futile to say any more to these people. They simply weren't going to accept any kind of evidence . . . none at all. This was their home and they were defending it. They were pulling the wagons into a circle.

"Well," Didi said sweetly, running her hands once through her hair, "I have rounds to make." And with that she walked out of the trailer and back into the parked jeep, Charlie close behind her.

"What are you going to do now, Miss Quinn?"

"What do you think I should do, Charlie?"

"I don't rightly know."

Didi sat silently at the wheel. A few seconds later Laz Runay exited the trailer and bowed slightly in her direction. Then Faulkner emerged and waved to her. Didi did not return either greeting.

She drummed her fingers on the steering wheel. She knew what she *wanted* to do. Keep her own counsel and get to the bottom of the matter. Do it herself. That was what she should do.

And if she was going to follow the dictates of her conscience, the first order of business was to find out who killed Ti Nolan.

Chapter 9

"How come you're not on rounds with Miss Quinn?" Mrs. Tunney asked Charlie as she refilled his coffee cup at the kitchen table. Didi had left in her jeep not five minutes before and Mrs. Tunney was hovering over him now, waiting for an answer.

"She ain't doing rounds," Charlie said. "She's going to the circus grounds."

"Well, why aren't you with her on the circus grounds—like you're supposed to be?" Mrs. Tunney persisted.

"She gave me the day off to take care of business."

"Ha! What kind of business do *you* have to take care of?"

"Why don't you go and do some work?" Charlie snapped.

"This is my kitchen! I'll do what I want here," she retorted.

Then Charlie realized that it would be a mistake to get on the wrong side of Mrs. Tunney today. So he just raised his hands and muttered that she could stay around and watch him conduct business if she wanted. Mrs. Tunney moved on, filling the cups of the other retainers.

Charlie turned his attention to Trent Tucker, who was sipping from his mug. "In about an hour," Charlie said, "Mrs. Sweet is going to be waiting for you in her car in the lot of that old boarded-up Carvel place. You know it?"

"Yeah," Tucker said. "It's just past the creek bridge."

"Right. Now you're going to give her two packages. And she's going to give you fifty dollars. You got that?"

Trent Tucker nodded.

Charlie got up from the table, walked into his bedroom through the narrow corridor and returned with two items. He put one on the kitchen table and one on the floor.

"Now this," he said, holding up an old hydrogen peroxide bottle, now filled with a viscose substance and closed in by a cork, "is for her dog's eyes. It's just a good wash of cucumber juice and sage and some other mush. You just tell her to wash the dog's eyes with it three times a day. Okay?"

Trent Tucker nodded.

"Mrs. Sweet's dog has cataracts. Only surgery will help him," said Abigail in a soft voice. All eyes turned toward her. Abigail rarely spoke. In fact she was practically a mute. Everyone knew that while she was a lovely young woman, her barn had burned down a long time ago. Everyone knew that as long as Abigail was ethereal and quiet, there was no trouble at all. But once in a while she seemed to lose all sense, like the time she took up with that terrible young hoodlum, who was now behind bars—and good riddance.

After the initial shock of her contribution to the discussion, everyone turned away from Abigail and ignored her outburst. Everyone, that is, except Mrs. Tunney, who said, "Abigail is no dummy. She's giving you a warning, Charlie Gravis. And you know what the warning is: Miss Quinn is going to throw a regular hissy fit if she finds out about what you're doing. She doesn't like all that hocus-pocus medicine of yours."

"Missy Quinn is not going to find out," Charlie replied. "And besides, there are a helluva lot of people who swear by what you call hocus-pocus." He paused and smiled a little. "On top of that, missus, we could all use a little cash, and Mrs. Sweet is going to give Trent here fifty big ones."

It had the wrong effect on Mrs. Tunney. Instead of being happy at the thought of cash, she became even saltier. "What cause have you got to complain, Charlie Gravis? Miss Quinn takes care of us as good as her mother did before her, God rest her."

"I never said Miss Quinn isn't good to us! But don't I deserve a good cigar once in a while? And shouldn't Trent here be able to fix his pickup? And what about some new church-going dresses for you and Abigail? What if she wants to take singing lessons again, or piano lessons? We all know that's the only thing she likes."

No one could reply to that feast of possibilities. Charlie proceeded with instructions for his second package.

He pulled it up from the floor and placed it gingerly in plain view on the table. He seemed to exhale proudly as he stared at it.

"Now this," he said proudly, "is not for Mrs. Sweet's pooch. It's for herself. It seems that she has a rash. A real bad one. She's an old woman now, and you all know how bad those things get."

"What is it?" Trent Tucker asked, staring at what looked like a sour cream container with string hanging over the sides.

"You just tell Mrs. Sweet that I took fresh risen cream, right out of the pail, and put it in a soft cotton sack and I buried it in the ground." He tapped the cylinder. "It came out of the ground just yesterday afternoon, all caked and rotted and ready to use. Tell her to just rub it in easy like. Once in the morning and once before she goes to bed. And just keep doing it till this is all used up."

He sat back expansively, pushing the glop toward Trent Tucker.

Suddenly Abigail spoke again: "Mrs. Sweet doesn't really have a skin rash. She has the shingles. It's caused by a virus. It has to be treated like a virus."

With that, Charlie lost his patience. He turned

toward her in a fury, but before he could say a word the telephone rang in Didi's office.

"I'm going to pick that up," Charlie said and left the table in a huff. Mrs. Tunney, Trent Tucker, and Abigail waited in silence for his return, each glancing from time to time at the two weird receptacles on the table.

Charlie returned in three minutes. He sat back down. "You'll never guess who that was." He waited for one of them to guess. No one did. No one even tried.

"It was a television station from Albany. They saw that photo of Miss Quinn in the paper and they want her to be on television. How do you like that?" Then he turned a harsh eye on Abigail. "I think you ought to go see how Sara and her litter's doing." Abigail, without another word, stood up and drifted out. Or rather, she glided out, for that was the way she moved and one of the reasons she spooked people so much.

"Now let's get back to business," Charlie said.

The two dancing girls were exercising together in the far end of the ring. Didi watched for a while before approaching. It was an eclectic routine: half ballet, half athletic warm-up. Linda Septiem was very pretty and a bit stocky. She wore a gray hooded sweater over black tights. Gwyn Masters was thinner, more supple, more like a dancer, and she had very long light brown hair, which swung loose as she moved. When the set was over and the girls were resting for a moment, Didi approached. "I'm very sorry to interrupt this," she said in a kindly but assertive tone, "but I just need a little of your time." They looked up, a bit startled, a bit confused.

"I want to ask you some questions about Ti Nolan."

"I thought you're a vet, not a cop," Linda Septiem said languidly and both of the dancing girls laughed. Didi did not laugh. But she wondered why Linda was so quick to think of the police. Was it just because there had been state troopers questioning everyone . . . or was it because she, too, felt that murder had been committed.

"In the week before her death, did Ti Nolan say anything to either of you that might make you believe she was afraid?" Didi asked.

Gwyn Masters shrugged. "You have the wrong girl here. Ti never told me anything about anything. We were not what you'd call friends." Gwyn raised one leg up to her outstretched arm and held it there in space.

Didi looked at Linda Septiem, who seemed to be contemplating the question with some seriousness. The dancer then laughed and shook her head. "Well, I guess if you're going to act like a police officer, then I am going to have to act like a perpetrator and confess. So here it is, Officer Nightbird, or whatever the hell your name is . . . and whatever the hell your profession is. My name is Linda Septiem. I knew Ti Nolan for two years. We were friends, sort of. She was born and raised in New Jersey. She went to Drew for about a year, then dropped out and became a dancer with a regional ballet company in Pennsylvania. She left that company, wandered around, and then joined the circus as a dancing girl, like many out-of-work ballet dancers do. If you can do a ballet barre, you can stand on the head of an elephant. As for me, Officer, I am not a ballerina. I am a tap dancer. That is all I know about Ti Nolan. And no, she didn't say anything the last two weeks of her life that sounded like she was afraid."

Linda Septiem stopped talking as suddenly as she had erupted. She swung violently into an exercise. Gywn turned on a small portable radio and the two girls began to coordinate their movements to the beat of heavy rap music.

I think, Didi thought, I did not make a good impression on these dancing girls. She turned and started to walk away slowly.

"One more thing!" Linda Septiem then called out, loud enough to be heard over the pounding music.

Didi turned, thankful for even scraps.

Linda started to speak but then she decided to make the encounter more personal. She left Gwyn and approached Didi, who was now in the center of the ring.

"Do you remember? You saw it! Didn't you? You were in the stands. It was right here. Right here! Remember!" Her voice was suddenly shaking and cloudy. It took a while but Didi finally realized that she was talking about that tragic matinee . . . that she was talking about the afternoon her friend had died.

But the dancing girl was wrong. "No," Didi said, "it was not here. Perhaps you didn't really see it. You were already out of the ring. Dolly just backed up into the ring again and then turned. Ti Nolan died over there." Didi pointed. "By the exit."

"So you say," the dancing girl said cryptically.

"Why don't you just stop playing this silly game and tell me exactly what you're thinking," Didi said.

"Why do that? Who the hell are you?"

"Listen, Linda," Didi answered calmly, using the young woman's first name for the first time, "if you were really a friend of Ti Nolan's you would want to help me. Because I'm the last friend Ti Nolan will ever have."

Linda's high-pitched laughter was wild, perverse. "How do you figure that?" she asked.

Didi took the plunge. "I think Ti Nolan was murdered and I'm going to find out who did it."

The comment seemed to puncture Linda's arrogance completely.

Didi turned and started for the exit.

"Wait!" Linda Septiem called out.

Didi turned back once more, waiting.

"Ti Nolan really had only one friend here. I mean only one good friend. And that was Topps."

"Who is Topps?"

"One of the Shelty Sisters. Topps Shelty. That's her name. Talk to her."

Three of the Shelty Sisters were pulling bags of equine vitamin supplement off a small truck and piling them fastidiously on the frozen ground. They didn't even see Didi approaching. They were caught up in the intensity of moving items that were actually too large for them to handle comfortably. The Shelty Sisters were fiercely independent; they spurned all use of roustabouts. They took care of themselves and their horses. They watered them and fed them and dealt with the bales of hay themselves.

Didi felt a growing sense of discomfort as she came closer to them. She had felt this way before. Miniature versions of what adults were "supposed" to look like, little people made her nervous—they were almost too perfectly formed. And they were so delicate, one always felt they were a step away from shattering.

"I am looking for Topps," Didi announced. The three sisters looked up from their chores.

"Topps is me," said one of them. Then she introduced the other two: "And this is Tina and this is Tillie."

It was difficult not to smile. All the Shelty's had a name that started with *T*. Up close to them, she also realized that there was a good possibility they were not literally sisters . . . that they called themselves a sister act but they were really just little people with shared talents banding together to make a living and practice an art. They surely didn't look alike up close. But she had never seen all five lined up.

"I'm Didi Nightingale, the veterinarian. I wonder if I could talk to you for a moment in private," Didi said to Topps.

"Oh, go talk to her," shouted Tillie. "Maybe you can get us some Nembutal."

"She's a vet, not a shrink," replied Tina.

Topps disengaged herself from her sisters and their chores and strode away from them. Didi caught up quickly and the two walked together.

"I would appreciate it if you told me what you know about Ti Nolan," Didi said. Topps Shelty stared at her wide-eyed for a moment. Didi added: "I'm trying to find out why she died."

The Shelty sister laughed bitterly. "She died because an elephant stepped on her head."

"Had you known her a long time?" Didi asked.

"Not that long. She used to come and watch us practice. She loved horses. She told me she used to ride a lot before she came here. Even won a blue ribbon at Ox Ridge."

"What kind of woman was she? I spoke to the other dancers but they couldn't really tell me who Ti Nolan was. Do you understand what I'm asking?"

Topps nodded. "She was hard to get to know. She stayed to herself. Read a lot. Listened to music a lot. Loved animals. She was a member of one of those animal-rights groups and was always sending them money. *Loved* the elephants. She was always buying them treats. Don't know anything about her family. Never met any."

Her words had been spoken very quietly and very quickly; all the Shelty Sisters seemed to speak like that—in a rush.

Didi felt a growing sense of frustration. She was not, she realized, asking the right questions.

"Do you know anyone who would have wanted her dead?" she asked bluntly.

Topps Shelty turned her exquisite tiny face up toward the larger woman. It was a pale face now and there were tears in her eyes. "Why would you ask such a thing?"

Didi didn't answer. She simply let her question resonate. But she was sorry that she had scraped an open wound: Topps was crying in earnest now.

"She was pretty," Topps said wistfully. "So pretty. Golden hair piled up on her head. High cheekbones. Long sloping shoulders. I never saw her dance ballet but she must have been wonderful. You could sense it."

"Do you know of anyone who would have wanted her dead?" Didi repeated the question deliberately.

For the second time, Topps ignored the question. "Once she made a party in her trailer. It was a birthday party, I think. But the only people who came were the other dancers and Lothar and myself."

"Did she know Lothar well?" Didi asked, trying to halt Topp's meandering.

"I think so. I think she knew few people but she knew them well . . . like me. She knew me well."

"Did she have friends outside the circus? Did she go visit them? Did she take vacations? Did she get phone calls? Please—every bit of information will help."

"Help?" queried Topps. "What kind of help can you give Ti now? She's beyond help."

Didi looked up. She realized that they were almost back where they started, near the busy tangle of little people. Topps had led her in a wide slow circle, back to her sisters. Just before she rejoined them, Topps indicated to Didi that she wanted to whisper something into her ear. Didi leaned down obligingly. The little woman said softly: "I think I understand it all now. Ti was really an heiress. You're a private dick in disguise as a country vet, hired by her attorney, who was really her long-lost father in disguise. He wants you to prove that Ti's wicked stepmother hired that hit woman elephant to kill Ti so she can get her hands on the estate. There's a big fee in it for you if you can crack the case. Have I got the story right?"

Didi stiffened, not at all happy to be made fun of. Without another word, she walked off in search of Lothar Strauss.

She found the big cat trainer high up in the stands of the main ring. He appeared to be watching the new elephant handler put his charges through their procession with the two remaining dancing girls on their backs. Strauss, as he watched, repainted the buttons on his performance outfit, which was now draped over his legs.

Didi had seen Lothar several times but had never spoken to him, and as she approached him, climbing through the bleachers, she became apprehensive. Strauss was an imposing man—in many respects. Not only because of what he did but because of how he looked and carried himself. He was a powerful man. Fast. He looked as if he could handle himself in any situation. He had, in fact, very much taken over the persona of his cats, but without their vulnerability.

Didi decided it was best to level the playing field right at the outset of the conversation, so she took on the kind of flippant attitude she would ordinarily not exhibit to a stranger: "Hello! Do you also do sewing?"

Lothar Strauss looked up from his labors. His eyes narrowed. He looked positively vengeful. Didi shivered a bit, wondering if she hadn't gone too far.

"What do I call a lady vet?" Lothar asked in a low, menacing voice.

"This lady vet is called Didi."

His menace dissolved all at once, the minute he smiled. "Well, Didi, yes. I do sew. In fact everyone in this godforsaken troupe does. You know why? Because we're poor. Now take those little Kingdom of Siam flags we sell . . . the ones with the white elephants on them. The kids love them. Why, we can't even afford to make them up individually in the U.S. No, they get sent here from Thailand in huge rolls and we have to cut the bolts into squares and then put them on the sticks. So we're all . . . seamstresses of a sort, Didi. And if you stay here long enough, it's a pretty good bet you'll have a needle and thread in your hands, too."

It was very funny thinking of the entire circus troupe seated in trailers making up those little flags with the white elephant logos. It was like some macabre quilting bee—Sheltys and Zappanus, fire eaters and top-hatted ringmasters, all sewing away.

Then Didi turned serious. "May I speak with you for a moment?" A formal question, a formal request, so that the big cat trainer would know she was not there just to chat.

"Of course," Lothar said, abandoning his tunic and leaning back in his seat with his hands clasped behind his neck like a conductor listening to a recording of his orchestra.

Didi came right to the point: "Topps Shelty told me that you were a particular friend of Ti Nolan." That wasn't really what Topps had said. She hadn't used the word "particular"; that was simply an embellishment that Didi thought might prove helpful.

She waited for Strauss to respond. He didn't say a word. He remained just as he was, hands behind his neck.

"That *is* what she told me," Didi prodded.

Lothar leaned forward suddenly and pointed with his thumb toward the ring. "That new man is pretty good. Very good."

Didi followed his finger. He was obviously talking about the new elephant handler.

She waited. Still Lothar did not address her remark about Ti Nolan. He seemed perfectly at ease sitting there in silence.

"Mr. Strauss, would you like me to leave?" she asked.

Strauss looked at her. "I was a friend of Ti Nolan's," he said simply. "So what? Were you her friend, too?"

"Of course not. I never met her."

"So now a lady who never even met Ti is asking about my friendship with her. How would you know if I was lying or telling the truth?"

"But why would you—or anyone—lie about being her friend?" Didi asked disingenuously.

"You keep asking those funny kind of questions, Didi. *How* questions . . . *why* questions. Like *How do those Bengals get my messages?* Like *Why do they listen to me?* He looked her full in the face then . . . hard. The thought came to her that his were the eyes of a snow leopard—hooded and gray—and terrifying.

"I don't like those questions," he said. "I really don't."

Lothar gazed down at his costume draped across his legs. He ran his hand along the fabric. And then suddenly the hardness of his face seemed to

dissolve and Didi saw a mask of sorrow so pro-
found that she had to look away.

Was that it? she thought. Had Lothar and Ti
Nolan been more than friends? Had they been
lovers? Was she talking to and watching a man
who could not bear the loss of his love?

"Questions to no purpose," he muttered.

She was about to assert that there certainly was
a purpose . . . that his lover had been murdered!
But she held back, out of sympathy for his grief
perhaps . . . or perhaps out of fear.

"Thank you for your time," she said and started
down the stairs. She had gone exactly nine steps when
she heard his voice loud and clear. "I will tell you
what you want to know." When she looked back at
him, he was regarding her calmly, very calmly indeed.

"It is really very simple, Didi. There is no need
for all this cat-and-mouse questioning. What you
want to know . . . what you should know . . . is that
Ti Nolan was in love with Tran Van Minh. And
that sweet, silly little man reciprocated with every
ounce of strength and passion he had."

Then he held his tunic up to the light and
snapped it once, as if to test its resiliency.

The revelation staggered Didi. She had to get
away from him, to go somewhere else . . . to think.
In a sense, her house of investigative cards had
come tumbling down.

It was not a place Didi would usually go, particularly for lunch. It was a large bar and grill across

from the Fishkill Mall. But she needed to sit calmly and think. And she was hungry. She took a booth and ordered a rare cheeseburger and a bottle of beer. She was the only one in the restaurant area, though the bar had five or six drinkers.

When the burger came she didn't eat it. And she left the drink untouched. The hunger was still there but her growing agitation and confusion were overwhelming it. If Lothar Strauss had told the truth—and she had no reason to believe he hadn't—Ti Nolan and Tran Van Minh had been very much in love.

And if that was the case, the scenario was clear. Clear and ugly. Clear and bathetic. Clear and stupid and bloody and one of those horrendous botched love stories that regularly crawl out of the newspapers and local TV news shows.

A stranger in a strange land (Tran) falls in love with a beautiful young woman (Ti). She reciprocates. Days of wine and roses. Not only does the young woman reciprocate emotionally and sexually, but she also rides one of the elephants that Tran cares for. It is the best of all possible worlds. And then a sudden withdrawal of the young woman's affections. The worm of jealousy appears.

Didi paused in her reconstruction of events. She reached out and drank from the long-necked bottle, then realized that it was a very unladylike gesture; she poured some beer in a glass, then was ashamed of herself for worrying about appearing unladylike, so she ignored the glass and drank from the bottle again. She picked up the fork and ate some of the cole slaw that accompanied the burger.

It was Tran who fed the doctored bran mash to the elephant his lover danced on. He wanted to hurt Ti, to kill her. And then, when he realized what he had done, when the full scope of his grief and loss surfaced, he killed himself. It was the oldest story in the world. A crime of passion. A crime of love gone bad.

Didi took a small bite of the cheeseburger. Not bad. It was rare. And the bun was delicious. She chewed slowly. It was all over now . . . the horror of what she had seen in the circus ring . . . and the horror of what she had seen in that bloody trailer. The memories were already dimming, muting.

She realized suddenly that her forehead was bathed in sweat. It was anxiety. But why? Everything was clear now. Horrendous but clear. The murderer was Tran Van Minh . . . that rather lovely man. She could not understand how a mind could become so twisted. She had had an experience something like his. She had loved a man greatly— a professor at Penn—Drew Pelletier. And then suddenly and with no explanation he had ended the affair, dumped her with no warning. She had experienced the hurt and the loss and the sense of aloneness . . . the feeling that this wound could never be healed. In an attempt to forget, she had run to India to study. She had done all kinds of stupid things. But, murder? Destroying the life of the one loved and then oneself—she could not understand that.

Didi pushed the plate away. She took another drink from the bottle and then pushed that away. She signaled to the waitress. She ordered a cup of coffee and a raspberry tart.

The pastry was delicious. Didi always had a weird sense of guilt when she ate a fruit tart or pie in the winter. Her mother would never do that. She ate fruit only in its season. But then again, the modern world had passed her mother by, or rather her mother ignored it. Up to the day of her death she thought no one should eat a fruit pie out of season—as if the world still cared whether pies were made from fresh-picked fruit.

God bless farm women, Didi thought. She paid her bill and headed for the door.

As she passed the bar, however, she stopped abruptly. Seated there was Allie Voegler. He wasn't alone. Next to him was a beautiful woman of about fifty. She had short white hair. She looked vaguely familiar. They were talking quietly to each other and looking at a piece of paper that Allie was holding up.

What, Didi thought, was Allie Voegler doing in Fishkill? This wasn't his jurisdiction. And what was he doing in a suit and tie? She felt a sudden flash of jealousy and then was ashamed of herself. After all, she had no claims on Allie. None at all. They were friends, not lovers. And difficult friends at that.

He hadn't seen her yet. She could just keep going out the door. No. That was no way to act.

"Hello, Allie," she said pleasantly.

He turned on his stool. "Didi!" He just stared at her.

"Yes, it's me, Allie," she said after a moment.

Finally he clambered off the stool and took a step toward her, but then stopped. "Oh, sorry . . . Didi Nightingale, this is May Dunlop." The woman nodded in a friendly manner. Yes, Didi knew who she was now: the banker's wife, from Hillsbrook.

There was an awkward silence. Allie looked absolutely miserable. Didi was having a hard time disguising how much that pleased her.

"Please . . . Didi . . . join us."

"Thank you but I can't. I have an appointment. Nice seeing you, Allie. And nice meeting you, Mrs. Dunlop."

Allie caught up with her just as she was opening the jeep door. The wind was blowing his wet combed hair to hell. He looked very unhappy.

"Wait, Didi, I just want to explain. It's not what you think."

She smiled at him. "Allie, I don't think anything. And you don't have to explain anything."

"But I see that look on your face. Listen, I'm here on business."

"Allright, you're here on business. Fine. I have to go."

"No, wait."

She waited. Why had this become such an unpleasant situation for both of them?

"I'm telling you the truth, Didi. I'm here on business. A bunch of kids broke into the Dunlop place a few nights ago. They took a lot of stuff. Then they dumped most of it. Seems they were on a real joyride. A kind of kiddie crime wave. They've been breaking into houses all over the county. Five or six big houses. They seem to like bank vice presidents and such. I got a call from the Fishkill police that some of the Dunlop valuables were thrown away around here. So May . . . Mrs. Dunlop . . . came out with me to identify the stuff."

"Okay. I believe you, Allie. But now I've *got* to go. Besides, we're acting like children. I don't care who you drink with. And you shouldn't have to explain."

Didi saw that May Dunlop had come out of the bar and was standing, relaxed, in the entrance. She is very elegant, Didi thought. Mrs. Dunlop was wearing light brown corduroy slacks, a darker brown sweater. No makeup and no jewelry except a pale blue brooch on the sweater with what seemed to be a white unicorn etched on the blue background. She wore low-cut stable boots. Yes, Didi thought, very much the wealthy horsewoman.

"What's going on at the circus from hell?" Allie asked.

She smiled. "You made it clear to me that you're not involved. And you don't want to be involved. You told me that it's out of your jurisdiction. If you will remember, you characterized my speculations as fanciful."

"Yes, I did, but—"

Didi cut him off. She climbed into the jeep and started the engine. "Anyway, Allie, it seems to be all resolved now. All the interested parties are dead. See you around."

Once home, she tried to busy herself with small tasks. There had been no emergencies. First she checked out Sara's litter. The piglets were doing fine—alert, squeaky, greedy. Then she started in on the files in her office, but that was just an impossible task, so she fled upstairs to her room. A pile of unread magazines beckoned to her. She started going through them, looking for articles that would interest her. Nothing did. She was slipping deeper and deeper into a depression. It was the tale of the doomed lovers—Tran and Ti—which so oppressed her, which kept stealing over her like a heavy cloak. She lay down on the bed and shut her eyes but sleep did not come.

A walk! she thought after half an hour. A brisk walk. That will fix me up. She threw on her big storm coat, scrunched a ski hat down on her head, slipped on a pair of fur-lined mittens and left the house. She trudged across the field and into the pine forest.

Her feet crackled against the residues of ice and snow on the ground. The boughs of the pines were still eerily laden with ice. The forest still frightened her, as it had when she was a child, but, paradoxically, it was the place she always came for repose.

A brilliant early afternoon winter sun had begun to burn through. Icicles melted and snapped. The sounds were like thunderclaps in her ears and they bothered her. She decided not to go deeper into the forest but to hover about the edges and watch for owls, even though they usually hunted only at night.

Didi saw no owls—only two red squirrels playing tag.

She made a slushy snowball and flung it straight up as high as she could. It dissolved on the way up and she slipped into a deep gloom again. The dissolution of the snowball was so quick and total that it reminded her of the dissolution of the love between Tran Van Minh and Ti Nolan.

Then she heard a strange sound, like an echo. At first she thought it was coming from deeper within the pines, but then she realized it was from without. She walked briskly out of the forest and stared across the field to the house. Yes, Charlie Gravis was there . . . calling to her.

When she was within ten feet of him, he said: "Agatha is sick."

"Who is Agatha?"

"One of the Bengal tigers at the circus."

Didi shook her head sadly. Well, maybe Thomas Allenbach had been right after all. His circus was in a cycle of some of the worst luck she'd ever seen.

Chapter 10

A very calm, very composed Lothar Strauss was waiting for them as they pulled in.

"You come with me, Charlie," Didi said as she climbed out.

"Thank you for showing up so quickly," Lothar said.

"That's what I'm paid to do," Didi retorted, and the moment she uttered the words she was sorry. She realized how nasty her tone was.

"I have her in one of the holding cages. You can examine her through the bars," Lothar said as the three of them hurried toward Agatha. Then he added: "Even I don't like to get into a cage with a sick Bengal."

The cage was secured on a flatbed truck. Didi approached it quickly and quietly.

"Oh my!" she exclaimed. She couldn't help herself. The 300-pound magnificent Bengal tiger was lying in that very peculiar yet recognizable position—forelegs folded under the chest and back arched. Oh, she had seen that position many times in house cats and it often meant big trouble.

"Is she eating?" Didi asked.

"No," Lothar replied emphatically.

"Water?"

"She seems to want water. She gets close but then she won't drink."

"Hmmm. A light fever. And her pulse is much weaker and much more rapid than normal. Any of the other tigers sick?"

"No."

Didi walked slowly back and forth around the three sides of the cage that were accessible on the truck. The cage was very small. She could reach in and stroke the big cat from any angle, but she did not.

"Any vomiting?"

"No," Strauss said, "but she has a funny smell in the mouth. Almost as if she had vomited."

"When did you notice she was sick?"

"It's hard to say. It happened very fast. She was fine early this morning."

"Well," Didi said slowly, keeping her eyes on the big cat as she spoke, "I'm afraid it *may* be feline panleukopenia."

"What the hell is that?"

"Kittens are routinely vaccinated against it nowadays," Didi answered almost academically.

"I asked you what the hell you're talking about."

"I'm sorry. I didn't mean to change the subject. It's a parvovirus."

"Parvo—Damn! You're talking about enteritis then!"

"Yes. It used to be called that." Didi tried to keep her voice level. It was obvious Lothar was close to exploding.

"What are you going to do?" he demanded.

She stared at the big cat. There was a protocol of treatment that the book prescribed: administer a parenteral antimicrobia . . . a balanced electrolyte solution . . . a Phenothiazine-derivative antiemetic. Didi knew what to do. The problem was—and it was a big problem—every vet worth his or her salt knew that 90 percent of the time the treatment was worthless. The patient died in five days no matter what you did or didn't do. Only once in a while did the animal recover. And that, too, happened no matter what the vet did or didn't do.

"I don't know yet," she said to Strauss.

Lothar began to pace nervously, staring at his great cat with both horror and sadness, as if he had somehow betrayed her and she knew it.

Didi added, "Besides, I'm not absolutely sure of my diagnosis." She began to circle the cage again. The symptoms of panleukopenia were sudden onset, pyrexia, anorexia, dehydration, vomiting, and diarrhea. Agatha exhibited some of those signs—and she was lying in that telltale position. But she was not at all dehydrated. And that was a key symptom.

Didi called Lothar over, asking him to come

close, both as a therapeutic attempt to get him out of his increasing agitation, and as a way to make her own thoughts clear.

"Look at her, Lothar. You see, there is virtually no dehydration. And dehydration always presents itself in this disorder."

"So?"

"So it may be simply a *subclinical* infection—which is rare with this disease. But it does happen. Or . . ."

"Or what?"

"Or it's not that at all."

"So what do we do?"

"Okay, first you should scrub down all the spaces that Agatha shared with the other cats."

"Scrub with what?"

"Any kind of dilution of household bleach. It's sodium hypochlorite."

"Then what?"

"Then just cover the cage. Keep her warm. Watch her. If there's no change by morning, I'll take some blood and send it to the lab."

Didi stepped back and allowed Lothar to do his work. The trainer set about scrubbing all the cages, covered the sick cage, set up a small tent half of which stretched out from the flatbed truck and provided him with shelter for his vigil.

"Why don't you sit with me for a while—both of you," Lothar requested. Didi and Charlie did as he asked. Lothar set out some upended barrels and all three were soon relatively snug under the tent half. Lothar wrapped an army surplus blanket around each of them. Then he set up a small table between them and placed a bottle of brandy on it, along with paper cups and a deck of cards.

"I thought," he explained, "that since you're kind enough to keep me company, I should show some hospitality."

There was no argument from Charlie. He took the deck and began to shuffle the cards. "How about rummy?" he asked. The other two agreed. Charlie dealt. For the first time in years, Didi was actually in a card game. She tried to concentrate. But her mind was on the tiger and on her own performance. Why hadn't she started treatment immediately? Was it only because the treatments rarely saved the patient? Or was it that the diagnosis was faulty? Without dehydration there is no parvovirus. But the tiger *was* presenting the other symptoms. Or most of them.

Maybe she was doing nothing, she realized, because of what the old vet in South Carolina had counseled when she'd had the sick elephant on her hands. Do nothing. Wait. Watch. As if it were an environmentally induced disorder.

The game proceeded. Charlie won. The next game went to Lothar. Dr. Nightingale failed to win a single game, and she couldn't have cared less. She kept peering up from the cards to observe the resting tiger. The liquor in the pear-shaped bottle diminished slowly but surely. They were all warm now with the blankets and the portable heater and the brandy and the camaraderie.

It was starting to get dark.

Another reason for her inactivity, therapeutically, came to Didi. A possible but embarrassing reason. Had she unconsciously absorbed the folk wisdom of all the dairy farmers she had grown up around? It was one of the folk beliefs of dairy farmers that there is absolutely no distinction between human and animal and even plant disease. When something was "going around," everyone and everything was at risk. If there was a blight on the tomato vines, that meant that sooner or later some children and some cows were going to get ill with some kind of bug. It was a very unscientific approach. Of course, scientists are only now beginning to understand that there are literally thousands of bacterial, fungal, and parasitic diseases of plants that affect animals, and of animals that attack humans. Didi squirmed. Was that it? She had done nothing with this sick tiger because she felt that "something was going around" the circus grounds. It had touched the elephant and now was touching the tiger. It was some kind of organism in some kind of feed and not all the therapeutics in the world could stop it or stay it. Just let it run its course.

"You don't seem to be too lucky at cards," Lothar said.

"I rarely play," Didi replied.

"Circus people play cards all the time. In fact, contrary to popular belief, the longest-running poker game in the world is in one of the back tents of the Ringling Brothers Circus. I hear it is now close to sixty years old—uninterrupted. That's dedication." Didi and Charlie laughed. It was good to listen to the big cat trainer, especially now that he seemed to have recovered his control.

"My sister," Charlie said, "used to play cards a lot. She lived in the western part of the state, near Jamestown. Good dairy country there. But she only liked solitaire. And it was the kind of solitaire I never saw before or since. She's dead, my sister. I don't know why I never asked her the name of the kind of solitaire she was playing."

"Maybe," Lothar suggested, "she wasn't playing cards at all in any real sense. Maybe she was just laying them out. Maybe it was just a nervous habit, like people playing with loose change."

"Could have been," Charlie agreed. He shuffled the deck flamboyantly and dealt again. Lothar refilled their paper cups with the excellent brandy.

Didi looked fondly at her companions. She was beginning to feel very good. And it was not only the brandy.

There, in the makeshift tent, in the cold and growing darkness, she felt like she was in Africa, on a safari, searching for some magnificent beast. Yes, before she wanted to become a veterinarian, Didi wanted to be an adventuress, an ex-

plorer, a discoverer of animal and plant species
that no one had ever seen. She had spent count-
less feverish hours as a child with several of her
mother's books by Martin and Osa Johnson, a
couple who were always returning from the wilds
of the Congo to write romantic books such as
African Adventure. Half fiction, half fact; filled
with miraculous escapes from enraged elephants; and tender ministrations for gorillas
wounded by evil poachers. Didi could not get
enough of them.

This feeling good . . . this gentle fantasy that she
was someplace else . . . ended abruptly when
Lothar Strauss, under the influence of too much
brandy, suddenly flung down his hand of cards,
buried his face in his hands and began to weep.
Charlie and Didi stared at each other, neither of
them knowing what to do. The tears came in se-
vere, great sobs; Lothar's body seemed to be in
spasm.

Then he wrenched himself out of his misery,
stared at Didi through red-rimmed eyes and asked:
"She is going to die, isn't she? Agatha is going to
die."

"I don't know. If it is enteritis," she said, using
his term, "then she probably will, Lothar." Didi
evaluated him, his misery; she had learned that
one must never soften the blow when it comes to
the death of a beloved animal. Tell the truth as you
know it. Do not spare the person, because it will
come back to haunt everyone. "But I don't know

what's bothering Agatha, Lothar. Right now . . . this
moment . . . I truly don't know."

"I don't want her to suffer. Do you understand
that? I raised her. I don't want her to be in any
pain."

"She's not in pain right now, Lothar. There has
been no real deterioration. There has been no dehydration. Discomfort perhaps, but not pain."

Strauss stared at her malevolently for a moment and then turned away. Didi realized that
the big cat trainer was used to dealing with old-
fashioned vets who accepted pain as a matter of
course. Didi was not like that. She was of the
new school who believed that pain caused shock
and shock negated any kind of therapy. So, Didi
would dispense pain killers at the drop of a hat if
safe. Of course, there was always a danger involved because pain killers could easily mask
symptoms and that could be fatal. But Didi always erred on the side of compassion. She always
remembered what her professor—Hiram Bechtold—had said, "You cannot feel another human's
pain. Nor can you have any inkling of the depth of
an animal's suffering. So you must always judge it
by the pain you yourself have felt in the past. If
you are a stoic and oblivious to pain . . . or a devout person and feel that suffering is a gift from
God—then, of course, you can let the animal suffer on the grounds that this, too, will pass. But if
you are an average person . . . as I am . . . alleviate

the pain you intuit in the other—be he animal or human. And do it quickly."

As if to atone for his weeping, Lothar Strauss then produced a bottle of red wine and some sickly sweet store-bought cookies. They started to play cards again, this time alternating between rummy, casino, poker, and blackjack.

Didi soon lost all interest in the cards and just watched dimly as Charlie and Lothar continued to play.

How odd this circus job has become, Didi mused. She had always considered herself a "hands-on" vet. Do something quick and if that doesn't work try something different. And keep trying until the animal is well.

But this was the second circus animal to come down with something on her watch, and for the second time she was doing absolutely nothing. It had worked with the elephant. Would it work with the big cat? Had she an option?

Didi realized for the first time why so few students graduating from veterinary school evinced an interest in zoo work. It was too difficult. Too much depended on a single move. There weren't flocks of elephants or herds of tigers. There were usually only one or two of each. Each was precious to the institution where it domiciled. Each had been procured at great cost. And they weren't domesticated animals. There was no corpus of scientific treatment on which the vet could operate. No wonder sometimes it was best to do nothing. A Bengal tiger was not a short-haired tabby. Not for the veterinarian.

A kind of delicious stupor came over her. She alternated between being slightly chilled and slightly too warm. She drifted off into sleep. The last thing she remembered was the thought that if she ever had grandchildren she could stay up with them one night and tell them tales about her "circus days."

Someone coughed. Didi opened her eyes. She remembered where she was. She sat up. Charlie's eyes were open. And across the makeshift table was Lothar Strauss. His eyes were opened, too.

Who had coughed? She didn't know. She sat up and looked at her wristwatch in the glow of the lamp. My God. It was almost midnight.

Then she heard the cough again. This time it was frightening. A kind of "Khuff . . . Khuff" . . . a deep resonating cough that seemed to come from the darkness. Didi shivered. She looked at Charlie. He seemed frightened. She looked at Lothar. He seemed puzzled.

The sound came again and Didi wrapped the blanket tighter.

But then she saw Lothar's eyes grow wide. And a second later it was he who coughed: "Khuff . . . Khuff."

An answering cough came back, and then Lothar whooped like a child finding a bright green bicycle under the tree on Christmas morning. He stood straight up, flung his blanket away, ran past Didi, pulled the tarpaulin off Agatha's holding cage and began to cough for all he was worth. Agatha coughed back. Soon the coughs took on the shape of a tune.

Didi grabbed the lantern and held it close to the cage. The big cat was up and about and beginning to slam against the sides of the narrow cage in an almost playful manner between conversational coughs.

And Agatha let out a deep-chested roar that seemed to shake the bars like corn sheaves.

"She's hungry! She's thirsty!" Lothar began to shout and did a ludicrous dance of joy around the cage.

"Damn!" was all Charlie Gravis could say.

Didi felt weak in the knees. She sat back down. She looked at her veterinary assistant. "It must have been a subclinical variant of the parvovirus," she explained.

"You mean a twelve-hour bug?"

"From your lips to God's ears, Charlie," she replied, using one of her mother's favorite recipes for hope.

Chapter 11

It was one of those upstate mornings that try police officer's souls. A steady icy rain had made the highways treacherously slick. Seven nonfatal accidents had kept Allie Voegler busy in his unmarked police car between the hours of six and nine.

Now it was nine-thirty and Allie was at his cramped desk trying to drink one full container of coffee without interruption.

Officer Storch came past and dropped the morning paper onto his desk. Allie nodded his thanks and opened it.

Right there on the front page was another story on Didi Quinn Nightingale, DVM. This one wasn't about an elephant. It was about a Bengal tiger.

LOCAL VET TACKLES TIGER TUMMYACHE, the headline read.

There was a picture of Didi and Charlie Gravis and what seemed to be the tiger's trainer circling the prostrate cat in a small cage lashed to a flatbed truck. It wasn't really a good picture of Didi. The one in the elephant story had been better. Allie smiled at the sight of her, but the smile turned quickly to a glower when he remembered that very strained chance meeting in the Fishkill bar.

It was time, he realized, that he started making a conscious effort to forget about her. Nothing was ever going to happen between them. The sooner he understood that the better. He stared at the picture for a long time. It would be very hard, he knew, to forget about her.

Reluctantly he pushed the paper away, finished his coffee and began to peruse the new sheaf of outstanding warrants issued by the FBI. It was a typical witches' brew of at-large felons—including bank robbers, drug dealers, arms smugglers, and many who had escaped from lawful Immigration Service confinement.

He began to leaf through them quickly; it was really a formality. Few outstanding warrants on these kinds of people were executed in Dutchess County. That was mainly because the New York State Thruway ran on the other side of the Hudson River. It was the preferred thoroughfare of felons moving back and forth from Canada.

Suddenly, a blur of a face caught his attention. He flipped back to find it.

No! He couldn't find it. He cursed under his breath and started to turn the sheets very slowly. He came to it. A thin, handsome Asian man was gazing at him from the page. Yes, no doubt, Allie had seen that face somewhere.

The name attached to the face was one Ieng Mok.

The sheet identified him as a Cambodian national of Vietnamese ancestry. He had entered the U.S. direct from a Thai refugee camp (Number 17), on a temporary visa for medical treatment. He had been sponsored by one of the American church groups administering the medical and relief services in the Thai camps.

In addition to being an illegal alien, he was wanted in connection with bank fraud, assault with a deadly weapon, and escape from lawful confinement.

The bottom of the sheet said that Ieng Mok should be considered armed and dangerous. His aliases included Johnny Dap and Tran Van Minh.

Allie exhaled, suddenly excited. Yes, now he remembered the name Tran Van Minh, and he remembered seeing the face in the newspaper. It was the elephant handler at the traveling circus who had committed suicide . . . the one who played such a large role in Didi's speculations about the drugged elephant.

He slipped the circular from its latch. The department owed him plenty of comp time. He could easily take the afternoon off and go to the circus matinee. He could give the circular to Didi. She would be very interested. She would be very grateful. It was a nice gesture. It would end this ridiculous tension between them . . . these bad feelings that had suddenly surfaced all because she had seen him with that woman in the bar. Yes, he thought, this is a very good idea. He folded the paper and slipped it into the pocket of his red-checked flannel shirt. He then adjusted the thick black tie he was wearing. An afternoon at the circus!

It was just past one when Allie paid his way into the big tent. The bleachers were already three-quarters full even though the matinee didn't start for another fifty minutes. Once inside, Allie seemed to let go of all his inhibitions. After all, he was off duty. First he had two frankfurters with mustard and onions. Then he had half a salt pretzel. Then he purchased one of the satin flags with the white prancing elephant on a green field.

His section was all the way up, so he didn't take his seat right away. Besides, he was looking for Didi. His eyes swept the crowd, but he didn't see her. No doubt she would be in some VIP box—after all, she had signed on as the circus vet—but he couldn't find anything that could be construed as special seating.

Two children rushed past him brandishing their circus programs. They half spun Allie around because their programs caught near the point where his hand held the tiny flag. Allie stepped back. More kids started to run. Allie saw a young woman near the exit. The kids were running to her. He didn't know who she was but it was obvious they were running to her for her autograph. Obviously a celebrity of some kind; maybe one of the circus performers.

Then, to his astonishment, he saw a familiar older man walk up to the sought-after celebrity. It was none other than old Charlie Gravis.

Allie stared at the celebrity again. Good Lord! It was Didi.

He just hadn't recognized her because she was dressed up. It was certainly a change from her usual jeans or overalls and woolly shirts and thick-soled boots. She was wearing a tight black skirt with a dramatic white ruffled blouse and a black vest. And high heels. Her hair was longer than he had remembered, and she was wearing bangs.

She looked beautiful. He was dazzled. He always knew she was pretty. But not like this. He had always appreciated her lovely figure—Didi was slim and strong with wide shoulders. But he had never seen her in a tight skirt. He didn't know what the hell to do. And then he pulled out the outstanding warrant sheet and got on line for an autograph. It took him a while, waiting on the line, to understand why anyone would be waiting for Didi's autograph. All those newspaper stories about the local vet saving the elephants and tigers had obviously turned Didi into a local heroine.

Didi, who by this time had become quite embarrassed about the matter, and who had dressed up strictly on a whim, was now signing anything thrust in front of her nose.

When Allie pushed the warrant sheet into her hand she had already started to make the first signature marks on Tran Van Minh's face. It startled her! She pulled the pencil down to her side and looked up.

"Allie! What are you doing?"

"Just lining up like everybody else for the famous lady's autograph," he said mockingly. But Didi was not listening. She was staring carefully into the face of the dead elephant trainer.

Then Didi waved off the other children on line, telling them there would be no more autographs. She grabbed Allie's arm and pulled him into an alcove by the side of the bleachers.

"What is this? Where did you get it?" she asked.

"It's a warrant sheet. Your elephant handler was a criminal of sorts. Read it, Didi."

She studied the words on the circular.

"I never saw you dressed like this," Allie said. Didi ignored him. She was deep into the warrant sheet. When she finished she folded it carefully and handed it back to Allie Voegler. "It was very kind of you to let me see that," she said. "I appreciate it very much."

"Did you know anything about him?" he asked.

"Not what was on that sheet. It never even crossed my mind that he was an illegal alien or wanted for crimes." Didi shook her head slowly, sadly. It was just another nail in the tragedy. It

made Tran Van Minh's behavior even more clear.
Not only had the woman he loved withdrawn her
love but he was under the added pressure of
being sought by the police; of living under an
alias. He was living in a pressure cooker. And it
finally blew.

"I'm getting a might tired, Miss Quinn. Do you
think we can sit down?" Charlie Gravis interjected.

"Of course, Charlie. I'm sorry." Didi turned to
Allie. "Where are you sitting?"

"Up there," he said, pointing high into the
stands.

"Sit with us. We have an extra seat."

In fact, they were the best seats in the house,
because they were right behind the north exit of
the tent; anyone could see the performers as they
entered and left. And the elephants were so close
that one could touch their hind legs when they
pranced into the ring.

Didi sat between Allie Voegler and Charlie
Gravis. "My hands ache from signing those stupid
autographs," she said. Then she added, "The funny
thing is, Allie, on both of those stories in the
paper, I never even saw the photographer."

"Everybody loves a vet," Allie said, and the moment he said it he realized it had come out wrong.
There was a little bitterness, perhaps scorn in the
inflection. He hadn't meant that. He could feel
Didi bristle next to him. "Can I get you a frank?"
he asked quickly.

"Some peanuts," she said.

Allie hailed a vendor who threw him the bag after he had thrown him the change. Didi ripped open the package and distributed the nuts to the right and left of her.

Soon all three of them were contentedly cracking and munching as the circus came to life.

The grand opening parade was as exciting as ever, even though Dolly was still quarantined and poor Ti Nolan was in her grave. The audience whooped and hollered as the computerized music picked up the tempo.

Then came a brief interlude where one of the clowns tried to ape the fire swallower only to get burned and have the seat of his pants ignite. He ran about the ring and eventually jumped into a portable pool of water, to the delight of the children.

Then out marched the Shelty Sisters on their sturdy ponies. It was a dazzling, fast-paced performance based on split-second precision between woman and horse. The little women leaped from pony to pony. They somersaulted onto the ponies and off again. They batted a beach ball from one end of the pony line to the other.

The accident happened when the ponies went into a figure-eight pattern.

It wasn't a serious accident. The last two ponies of each crossing line collided.

There was a sudden gasp from the audience.

The ponies staggered . . . their knees buckling . . . but they didn't fall.

In fact they immediately recovered and fell back into the line of march.

The music was turned up louder. The audience applauded. The Shelty Sisters waved to their fans.

And the ponies then went into their final circling gallop at high speed while the Sheltys leaped from one to another of the horses like dervishes.

The act exited the ring to enormous applause. The clowns returned.

"I think I better have a look at those ponies," Didi said, standing.

Charlie groaned but stood up to accompany his boss.

"Can I come along?" Allie asked.

"Sure."

They headed out of the ring area to the half-open run that was formed between the back of the bleachers and the massive tent pegs.

The ponies were standing quietly, the steam from their breath rising in currents. The Shelty Sisters were beside them, sweaters and jackets already thrown over their own sweating bodies. Several of the little people held blankets with which to cover the ponies as soon as they cooled down. Two of the sisters stood enjoying a smoke.

Didi walked quickly over to Topps, the only Shelty Sister she had ever spoken to previously.

"Is everything okay?" she asked.

"Just fine," little Topps replied.

"I mean with your ponies," Didi said by way of clarification.

"Just fine!"

"Well, I thought I ought to take a look. There *was* a slight collision. We saw the knees buckle in the audience." Didi started to walk past Topps, who suddenly shifted over and blocked her way.

Another Shelty moved close to Topps. "We take care of our own ponies," she said. Didi looked at the two of them as if they were crazy. She just didn't know what to do.

"Look," she finally said in a kindly voice, "it's my job, you know. That's what I'm paid to do. I just want to look at them. I won't treat them without your approval."

Another Shelty sister joined the line of resistance and began to shout at Didi.

"What the hell is going on here?" a voice boomed out. And Thomas Allenbach shouldered his way between the warring parties.

"There was a collision in the ring. I want to look at the ponies," Didi explained. Her voice was beginning to tremble.

There was a long silence. Then Allenbach took Didi by the arm and led her a few feet away.

"I'm afraid that's not possible," he said. "The Sheltys have never let any vet look at their ponies."

A voice inside Didi told her: Quit! Quit now!

Don't accept this nonsense! Just walk out and don't come back!

Enraged, she turned on Allenbach to tell him what he could do with his job.

But then, suddenly, a stab of memory stopped her. It had emerged from her unconscious with such rapidity and such force that she started to babble. Then she caught hold of herself. Her behavior changed entirely. She smiled sweetly at Thomas Allenbach and said, "No problem. If the Shelty Sisters prefer not to use my services . . . it's definitely their decision to make."

She motioned to Charlie and Allie and the three of them walked away.

When they were out of earshot of Allenbach and the little people, she said to Charlie, "Why don't you take the jeep and drive back to the house. I have some things to clear up but I don't need any help. Allie can drop me off at the house when I'm done." She turned to Voegler: "Can you?"

"Of course," he replied. "I'm off duty." Even if he'd been on duty he would have said yes, because it was obvious Didi wanted to get rid of her geri-atric assistant for one reason or another.

They watched a happy Charlie Gravis drive off.

"You were very strange back there," Allie noted. "You looked like you were going to take that man's head off, and then, suddenly, you switched gears . . . and were just as sweet as pie."

"I *was* furious. I *was* going to quit on the spot. But then I remembered something."

"What?"

"That Ti Nolan was active in an animal-rights group."

"That dancer?"

"Yes, Allie, the dead dancing girl. Yes, I had her death all figured out in my mind. I had the whole tragedy solved. The elephant trainer and the dancing girl were lovers. Doomed lovers. That has been corroborated. So it all seemed clear. A typical crazed story of a break-up. A true crime of passion. Tran could not bear to lose his beautiful Ti. But she, for some reason, was growing tired of him, or was seeing someone else. So he doctored the bran mash of her mount. Maybe not to kill her . . . maybe just to scare her. I don't know. And then, when the worst happened, the guilt corroded his reason and he killed himself. Yes, it all seemed clear to me. And when you showed me that warrant for Tran, it made that scenario seem even more logical. Outlaws are desperate people, particularly an outlaw in love."

Didi paused and scraped her boot into the earth. "But now, Allie, I don't know. This thing with the ponies is so strange."

"You've lost me, Didi."

"I mean, what if Ti Nolan uncovered a pattern of animal abuse at this circus? If she did and could prove it, the circus would be shut down. What if that was the reason that Tran Van Minh murdered Ti Nolan?"

"It doesn't really matter, Didi. All the players are dead."

"But we don't really know that. Maybe Tran didn't act alone."

"So what are you going to do?"

"Look at those ponies."

"But they won't let you."

"At around five o'clock—about an hour after the matinee ends—all the circus people go to their trailers to eat. I'll examine the horses then."

"You can't do that, Didi!" he warned, visibly upset.

"Why not?"

"Well . . . because . . . it's . . . it's trespassing, I imagine."

"You're confused, Allie. I'm the resident vet here. No one told me about any restrictions when I took the job. No one put any restrictions on my rounds at all. I'll go visit any animal in the circus at whatever time I wish."

"Look, Didi. You do what you want."

"I'll need your help, Allie."

He looked at her suspiciously.

"You're not on duty now, Officer Voegler. What kind of trouble can you get into? We'll just be looking at some ponies whose owners don't want them to be looked at. That's all, Allie. It's not a felony. Hardly even a misdemeanor. Or conduct unbecoming a member of the Hillsbrook police force. You can't be brought up on charges for that."

"Okay. Okay. What do you need?"

"I need you to be fast and quiet."

Chapter 12

It was already dark. The lights in the trailers gleamed. The staff people and the performers were eating, exhausted from the matinee.

Didi led Allie Voegler into the semienclosed stable area. It was totally deserted except for the ponies and one stable cat who glowered at them.

Two bare overhead bulbs threw insufficient light on the space. The ponies looked like thickset greyhounds waiting for a mechanical rabbit. A long taut rope stretched the length of the stable. Each pony was tethered to this main rope.

"It will only take a few minutes if we work together," Didi whispered.

"I'm ready," Allie replied.

"All I'm going to do is pick up and flex the front legs of each pony. One at a time. I'm interested in the middle carpal bone."

"What is that?"

"The knee. In those kinds of collisions there are often bits of bone broken loose and floating."

"You mean bone chips?"

"Exactly."

"I had them in my elbow once . . . when I was playing football."

"A lot of people do," Didi noted, still whispering. Then she asked, "Do you have the sugar cubes?"

"Yes," Allie replied, "in my pocket."

"When we get to each pony you feed the sugar cubes and shine the flash down so I can see what I'm doing. Right?"

"How do I feed the cubes? Just shove them into the pony's mouth . . . like a baby?"

"No. Leave a few in your open palm and let the pony feed from your hand."

"Okay."

"Remember, Allie. These ponies have no cause to be frightened of us, as long as you don't make any sudden, jerky moves. Just do everything slow and steady."

"Before you wanted me to be fast and quiet, Didi. Now it's slow and steady. Make up your mind."

Didi didn't think that was funny. She headed toward the first tethered pony. Then she stopped, holding up her hand. She noticed that each pony's bridle was hung over the main tether line. She smiled at the sight of them. The bridles were festooned with decorations. Just like little girls who show horses always pin the ribbons on their horses' bridles—so the Shelty Sisters pinned their mounts. But they weren't show ponies . . . they were circus ponies . . . and the decorations included old political campaign buttons, small pieces of animal jewelry such as elephants and tigers and bears and unicorns—even a few broken strands of old pearl necklaces. The Shelty Sisters, she thought, had many childlike traits. Oh dear! Didi shook her head. What a patronizing attitude she was developing toward them.

Didi then went to work. Allie fed the sugar cubes and provided the light. Didi flexed the ponies' legs. She moved quickly from the first horse to the second to the third without any problem whatsoever. Not a single bite or buck. No lashing out. No backing up. Perfect ladies and gentlemen all—with sound knees.

Then Allie dropped the flashlight. He reached for it immediately but one of the ponies became playful and sent it rolling along with a pony hoof shot. Allie cursed. The flashlight stopped rolling in the aisle. Allie pursued it.

Then the screams came.

Screams so horrible . . . so filled with pain and terror . . . so clear and cutting . . . that Didi felt as if her spine was shriveling. She turned pale in the semidarkness.

Allie Voegler, after a moment's paralysis, reached down to his ankle holster and removed a small .32-caliber handgun. Then he sprinted out of the stable.

For a moment Didi could not follow. The screams sucked the strength from her legs. Then the ponies began to snort and stomp. They pulled at their ropes and backed into one another. "Whoa! Whoa!" Didi called out to them and just the mere speaking of those words gave her strength . . . gave her direction. She turned and ran out after Allie Voegler.

The circus grounds had become a madhouse. People were running. Lights were blinking. And behind them, over them, under them, were the screams . . . quieter now, higher pitched, more threatening.

"The cage! The tigers' cage!" someone shouted. Allie saw the cage about fifty yards away. He saw the blur of tigers.

A man rushed up to Allie. "Kill them! Shoot them!" he screamed in his ear.

Allie reached the cage. The screams had become a gurgle. The tigers were playing with something . . . batting it back and forth.

"Shoot them! Save her!" someone screamed in Allie's ear.

Then he saw that it wasn't a ball they were batting about. It was a human being. What was left of one.

Allie positioned himself to fire.

Suddenly a hand shot out and knocked his gun hand out of position. A man rushed past him and climbed into the cage. "No! No, Lothar!" people screamed. But Lothar Strauss was now into the cage among the tigers, taking their plaything away. They were not happy. The cage erupted in a cacophony of snarls and roars. But Lothar drove them back and soon all but three big cats lay panting and contrite along the perimeter of the cage. Lothar stood over the mutilated corpse of the second dancing girl, Linda Septiem. He stared down at her. One arm had been severed and half of her cranium chewed away. Oddly, there wasn't much blood.

Lothar began to babble. "Look what my babies have done. Look what my babies have done." He kept repeating that phrase over and over again, sometimes interspersing it with "They are going to put my babies down."

Allie heard the shriek of sirens drawing near. Someone had already made the call. But it was too late for the girl, he knew. He placed his weapon back in his holster. A woman spoke in his ear when he straightened up: "She tried to give the tigers a little treat. That's what probably happened. And they pulled her into the cage. She must have opened the latch. She must have dropped something and tried to retrieve it." Another bystander heard the analyzer and contradicted her in louder terms: "Someone threw her into the cage! You can bet on that." And then a screaming match ensued and Allie walked quickly away. Where was Didi? he thought.

Two circus roustabouts bravely rushed past him with a makeshift stretcher. They climbed into the cage, pushing Lothar Strauss to one side, and brought the body out. Some people rushed up to see the horror. Others turned away.

Then Allie saw Didi standing alone by the side of a trailer. One of her hands was touching the trailer wall, as if for support. Her other hand held the flashlight he had dropped in the stable area.

He walked quickly over to her. She didn't look well. Even in the flickering light he could see her pallor.

"It's one corpse too many," she said to him quietly, almost apologetically.

They watched together in silence as the police and EMS workers arrived. "I never heard such screaming," Didi said finally. Then she grabbed Allie's arm tightly, as if for support. It was an uncommon gesture for Didi.

"Are you okay?" he asked, concerned.

"A bit woozy," she admitted.

"Let's get out of here for a while. Let's take a drive."

They walked slowly to his car and climbed in.

Allie Voegler kept his vehicle well below the speed limit. He opened the driver's seat window and the cold air that rushed in was soothing. He stole glances at Didi from time to time as he drove in random circles. She had her seat belt on. She seemed composed. But he sensed the turmoil in her. It was her posture that gave her away, which signaled she was in some kind of shock—she was just sitting too straight.

He kept driving until he saw the posture soften a bit. Then he asked: "Why don't we go to that bar in Fishkill and get something to eat. Or drink?"

"Fine with me," Didi said.

He pulled the car into the lot adjoining the bar and grill.

As they exited he called out to Didi. "Do you want to leave your book in the back? Or should I put it in the trunk?" Allie had just noticed the large book on the back seat. He assumed it was Didi's.

"What book?"

"There," he said, pointing to the back seat.

Didi peered in. "Not mine," she said.

Allie opened the back door. The car light illuminated the large, dog-eared coffee table book. "Look! There's a bunch of pills there, too. You see them?"

"I see them," Didi said. She reached in and plucked the small vial off the seat. Holding it up to the car light she read the label.

"It's a well-known brand of corticosteroid. Administered orally. Veterinarians use it all the time. It's become almost the universal elixir."

"Then it's yours?" a confused Allie asked.

"No. It isn't." She looked at the bottle again. "Well, I use corticosteroids from time to time. But sparingly. For example, a lot of vets use it to clear up 'hot spots.' I don't. There are always side effects. Besides, it's primarily an anti-inflammatory agent. For all kinds of arthritic problems. And also for . . ." She paused, realizing she was starting to lecture Allie. "Anyway, it's a ubiquitous drug . . . but this isn't mine."

"And the book?"

Didi pocketed the vial. She picked up the large book from the seat and held it to the light.

The title was: *Elephants in Fact and Fancy*.

The subtitle was: *From antiquity to modern times*.

She flipped quickly through the pages—chock full of photographs and reproductions of old drawings, paintings, and book illustrations.

Then she saw the bookplate on the inside cover—an old-fashioned bookplate with an elaborate flower border.

The name on the bookplate was Ti Nolan.

Didi shivered. This was Ti Nolan's book. She showed the bookplate to Allie.

"How did this get into my car?"

"Maybe Linda Septiem put it there. Before she was thrown or pushed or fell into the tigers' cage. Maybe the book and the vial have something to do with the whole mess and whoever put it in your car, Allie, was trying to tell us something or give us something. And maybe Linda Septiem committed suicide by climbing into that cage. Maybe. Maybe, in fact, it was really Linda Septiem and Tran Van Minh who were in love. Or maybe Linda Septiem was really an undercover vet working for a radical animal liberation group. Maybe." Didi shut up . . . realizing that she was beginning to sound deranged.

Trying to calm herself, she closed the book quietly and tucked it under her arm.

Inside the restaurant, they took a booth. Didi ordered a Caesar salad and a glass of wine. She was still pale and jumpy from the screams. It was the screaming, not the corpse, which had unhinged her. She knew that and it was perplexing.

Allie ordered chopped sirloin steak and a bottle of beer. When the food was served he began to eat immediately. Didi ignored the food. She slowly leafed through the elephant book . . . gingerly . . . carefully . . . as if with each page turned there was a possibility that a scream would emerge . . . as if the pages were booby trapped.

"Do you realize, Didi," Allie commented, "that one-fifth of that entire circus is now dead? Right? I don't think that circus employs more than fifteen people. I mean on staff. And now three are dead. Right? And we're talking about all this happening in less than a week. It's incredible!" He went back to his food.

Didi paused in front of a reproduction of an Indian wall painting of the beautiful Queen Sirimahamaya.

She knew the legend well. The lovely queen has a dream. In the dream she has been whisked away to a magnificent wilderness castle and sequestered in an elegant chamber. She is visited there by a white elephant with a lotus flower in his trunk. The queen is awakened suddenly from her dream by the call of a bird. She discovers that she is pregnant and that the baby growing in her womb is Gautema Buddha.

Didi smiled. She was beginning to feel better . . . calmer. Thank you, Queen Sirimahamaya, she said to herself. She started to turn the page and stopped. Odd! The first four letters of the queen's name seemed to fascinate her.

She covered the remaining eight letters with her index finger.

What was left was "Siri."

"Allie, take a look!" she said, turning the book around and pushing it toward him. "Look at this name."

"It's a long one," he replied.

She placed a napkin over the last eight letters. "Now look at it!" she ordered.

"Okay. I'm looking. It's Queen Siri now."

"Tran Van Minh had written the letters S . . . I . . . R . . . I . . . in blood on the wall before he died."

"You mean he was trying to write the entire name of the queen out? But why?"

"I don't know. He probably knew the legend. All Buddhists do. Just as Christians know how the Virgin Mary became pregnant. If, in fact, he was a Buddhist."

"Well, we know he was a felon."

Didi pulled the book back and closed it. Another sad, inexplicable fact.

Allie started to laugh.

"What's so funny?" she demanded. She didn't think humor was appropriate given what they had witnessed less than two hours ago.

"I was just thinking about when you saw me at the bar in this place with May Dunlop. You looked angry. You looked jealous."

"And you enjoyed the fact that I looked jealous?" Her tone was bitter, accusatory.

"Oh come on now, Didi! I didn't say that. I didn't mean that."

Didi sat back and took a sip of her wine, holding the glass at the edge of the table with both hands along the stem.

"She is a handsome woman," Didi said.

"That's for sure," Allie agreed. He had a twinkle in his eye as if not only was May Dunlop handsome but she was enough to prove the point that older women are more desirable than younger ones.

"Elegant, in fact, in her expensive, throwaway, horsey clothes. I bet that sweater was pure cashmere," Didi said, remembering how May Dunlop had looked as she stood in front of the bar watching them talk.

Suddenly Didi uttered a groan of disgust and pushed the glass of wine so savagely toward the center of the table that half of the contents sloshed out onto the food.

"What the hell's got into you?" Allie asked, alarmed. "Is something wrong with that wine?"

"Not the wine," she groaned. "With me. Me!"

"You're acting crazy, Didi."

"Listen, Allie. I remember something very important. Pay the waitress! We have to get out of here. You have to drive me back to the circus now."

"But I haven't finished eating."

"Please, Allie. Pay the waitress and let's go."

Grumbling, he called for the check, paid, and drove Didi back to the circus grounds.

"Park away from the lights," she ordered. Allie followed her instructions.

"Wait for me here," she said. "I'll be back in five minutes."

"Where are you going?"

"Back to those ponies. Don't worry, Allie. Just wait here."

She vanished into the darkness and was back in the car in about three minutes—breathless and chilled.

"That was fast."

"Look at this, Allie!" Didi thrust a small object into his hand.

He flicked on the interior car light. "Damn! It's one of the unicorn pins taken with other junk from the Dunlop house. May collects them. She was wearing one the other day. Where did you get it?"

"It was pinned to one of those pony bridles."

Allie burst out laughing. "Do you mean it was those little women who trashed all the local homes? Can you imagine that? Little women with six-packs, breaking into houses for drunken orgies. Didi, let's face facts. If so many people hadn't died, your circus would be a Three Stooges operation."

"No, Allie, you got it wrong. I think it's more like Murder, Incorporated."

Her analogy made him nervous. "Are you serious?" he asked.

"Quite serious. Did you ever know a veterinarian to joke about life and death?" It was a rhetorical question and she didn't wait for him to answer. "Tell me, Allie . . . is there such a thing as professional courtesy among police officers?"

"Sure."

"Then you can call a police department in another city and get information on crimes in their jurisdictions."

"Of course. It happens every day."

"What if you make the request in an unofficial capacity?"

"Why would I do that?"

"I can think of a lot of reasons."

"What do you want me to do, Didi? What are you up to?"

She took the unicorn pin from him and tucked it into her pocket. "I want you to come home with me. I want you to make some calls from the phone in my clinic."

"Who to?"

"To the police departments of Jamestown, New York, and Scranton and Harrisburg, Pennsylvania."

"Why?"

"Because, according to the circus manager, those were the last three locations the circus performed in before coming here."

"But what am I looking for?"

"Simple, Allie. Murder. Suicide. Dismember-ment. Extortion. Arson. Brutality. Rape. Any may-hem whatsoever that coincided with the circus's stay in that location."

"Look, Didi, why don't we wait until I get to headquarters tomorrow morning? I can request the information through official channels."

"You and I know that wouldn't be wise, Allie. As you said, it isn't your jurisdiction."

"I don't know, Didi. I think you're just spinning your wheels. I think that tiger cage put you in shock."

"Then help me get out of that shock, Allie. Make the calls."

He could not withstand her plea. He started the engine and drove her home.

The moment Didi and Allie entered the kitchen, her elves gave the police officer all kinds of dirty looks and quickly relocated themselves elsewhere.

Mrs. Tunney, however, went directly to her room and slammed the door shut.

"They sure don't like me visiting," Allie said, grinning.

"I think they have other romantic plans for me," Didi explained.

"You mean I'm socially unacceptable?"

"Your daddy wasn't a dairy farmer," Didi said. Then Didi led him into the clinic office.

"I'll be in the kitchen, Allie, making coffee. There's a pad and pencil on the desk."

"What were those cities again?" he asked.

She repeated the Jamestown, Scranton, Harrisburg litany and then walked back through the long corridor and into the kitchen. She saw that the light in Mrs. Tunney's room was already out.

Then she lay the elephant book, the vial of oral corticosteroid, and the unicorn pin on the long kitchen table. She noticed an open box of expensive cigars there, too. Not the usual ones that Charlie smoked. He must, she thought, have gotten them as a gift. She closed the box and placed it on the counter. She started making a pot of coffee. She filled the pot with water up to the arrow. She measured out six tablespoons of A&P French Roast. She covered the pot and set it on a low flame.

Then Didi sat down to wait. She would bring Allie a cup when it was finished. The phone could keep him busy in the clinic for an hour at least, she figured.

The coffee began to brew. The smell was delicious. She heard steps in the corridor and grinned. It had to be Mrs. Tunney who had smelled the coffee in her room and decided to check out who was brewing coffee in her pot in her kitchen.

But it wasn't Mrs. Tunney. It was Allie. And she hadn't even laid out the cups and the sugar and the half-and-half yet.

He didn't look, though, like he wanted coffee. He looked troubled.

"What's the matter, Allie? They wouldn't help out?"

"No, Didi. They were very helpful . . . very professional. The problem, Didi, is that your circus never set up their tents in any of those cities or their environs."

Chapter 13

It was 9:03 the next morning when Allie saw Didi again. She was walking briskly down Main Street in the town wearing her work clothes. He honked his horn three times but she didn't stop. Then he rolled down the window and shouted her name out.

"Good morning, Allie," she said briskly and approached the car by the driver's side.

"After I left your house last night I checked out the state trooper report on the tiger cage. It's just a preliminary report but it seemed to imply an accident. The Septiem girl was feeding the tigers from the outside. Her jacket got caught. She opened the cage door to release it and one of the cats dragged her in. The report says the cage door is usually padlocked but the trainer had forgot to do it that evening."

Didi listened blankly and when Allie was finished said: "Well, thanks, Allie. I appreciate it."

"You don't sound too enthused by the report," he noted.

"If I believed that report, then I would also have to believe that you can cure tuberculosis by eating the butter churned from the milk of a cow that grazes in churchyards."

She smiled at Allie and then started to walk away.

"Wait a minute, Didi! Have a cup of coffee with me. What's your rush? Are you mad at me for something?"

She stopped, turned back and asked: "Why should I be mad at you, Allie?"

"Well, I don't know. Maybe you were mad at me because of the telephones. But it wasn't my fault. Right? Allenbach lied to you. They never played Jamestown or Scranton or Harrisburg."

"I have an appointment at the bank," she explained.

"They're open until three."

"I have an appointment with Charles Dunlop."

"What are you up to, Didi?"

"I'm going to question him about the circus."

"You mean because you found his wife's pin hung on a pony bridle?" Allie's voice was aggressive and contemptuous. Didi walked angrily back close to the driver's seat window.

"Do you have a minute, Allie?"

"More than a minute."

"Well, good. Because I'm going to give you a small lesson in veterinary medicine."

"Save it, Dr. Nightingale. I'm very unsophisticated in the realm of medicine and science."

"I don't think so. I think you know enough to wear a condom when you fornicate . . . don't you, Allie?"

His ears turned scarlet. He started the engine preparatory to driving off. The anger was evident.

"I'm sorry, Allie, I'm sorry. Calm down. Let me tell you something."

Allie cut the engine. He listened.

"One of my first clients when I came back here to practice was a young farmer in Millersville. He had a small but very healthy and very productive milk herd. Everything was peaches and cream, Allie. For him and for me and for the cows. Then, one day, one of the cows got sick. Not bad sick but the milk was stringy. And there were some boils on the udders and then some eye inflammation. A week later another cow took sick. And then another. I couldn't figure out what it was. I took blood samples and stool sample and tissue samples. I sent them to lab after lab, but no one could find anything. I couldn't make an intelligent diagnosis. Oh, it was obvious to me that some kind of microorganism was wrecking havoc. Maybe a virus. Maybe some kind of parasite in that very complex digestive system.

"I was stymied. So I treated 'as if.' I didn't know what I was doing. I administered antibiotics to start and then a host of other treatments. The cows kept getting sick. The farmer grew angry with me . . . fired me . . . and hired in my place a quote more experienced unquote veterinarian. He didn't do any better. When half the herd was sick, the farmer decided to send the entire herd to the slaughterhouse and then sold his farm.

"Six months later the farmer was arrested in some kind of bizarre charity fraud. A lot of interesting things came out in the trial. The most interesting being this: the farmer, unknown to me, had run up enormous gambling debts. He decided the only way out was to dramatically increase milk yield. He obtained from his feed dealer a new kind of designer hormone that hadn't even been fully tested. He administered it to his herd and never told me. Only his feed dealer knew."

Didi paused. "Do you understand what I'm saying, Allie?"

"Vaguely. That the horrors of what happened in the circus are not internal parasites."

"Correct. Not jealousy . . . not romantic angst. Something else, Allie."

"And Charles Dunlop is the feed dealer?"

"I don't know. But it's about money. It's about greed. I feel it, Allie, I know it."

"But why a bank executive?"

"Because of the unicorn pin. And because you told me that most of the houses that were broken into were those of bank employees."

"Yes, I did tell you that, Didi. And it's true. But it could have been a coincidence."

"It very well could be."

"What are you going to ask Dunlop?"

"Simple, Allie. Does he have any relationship to the circus? If so, what is it?"

"Why don't you meet me at the diner at around eleven and let me know his answer," Allie suggested.

"I'll be there," Didi said. She started to walk away, then stopped. "Is there any way you can think of to find out where that circus really performed before it came here?"

Allie pondered the question, beating with his fingers on the steering wheel. Then his face lit up. "Of course! They are using wide bed trucks; they're carrying heavy loads; and they're transporting wild animals on turnpikes and interstates. They need all kinds of special permits from the DOT and the ICC."

"I don't want to get you in any trouble," she cautioned.

"No trouble at all. We're plugged into the DOT computer. I'll find out."

"The diner at eleven?"

"Yes!"

Then Allie Voegler climbed out of his unmarked police car, resting his head on his arm, which was propped against the hood, and watched Didi Quinn Nightingale walk casually through the old revolving doors of the bank.

Charles Dunlop sprang up from behind his desk to greet her. He was still athletic and very well preserved for his age. A handsome, virile, successful man in a banker's suit with a starched blue shirt.

"It's not often we get a celebrity in this bank," he said. Then he laughed.

Didi sat down across from him. There was a neat desk between them, one that had recently been polished. The odor, not unpleasant, clung to the wood. Charles Dunlop's face saddened. "How proud your mother would have been, Didi, if she could have seen those stories about you in the press."

Didi folded her hands. She remembered that it was Charles Dunlop who had approved the loan to her mother in order to make that last addition to the house—rooms for her charges and the large storage shed that Didi had subsequently converted into the small animal clinic and office for herself.

"How can I help you?" Dunlop asked, sitting back down and transforming himself into the objective banker—quickly.

Didi had formulated her opening gambit before she entered the bank—and she delivered it flawlessly.

"You know that I was hired as the circus's veterinary consultant?" she asked.

"Well, I assumed as much from the newspaper stories."

She delivered the second line in the scenario almost sheepishly: "Do they have an account at this bank?"

"Yes, they opened a small account for their receipts. And to pay for local services," Dunlop replied. Then he added, "It's a short-time account. The standard kind of thing. Very little money involved. We issued them a limited number of checks."

Suddenly his face lit up and he sat back expansively. He now understood the reason for her visit, or believed that he did. Didi was in the bank because she was afraid she wouldn't be paid for her services.

"There has been no trouble at all," Dunlop said, alluding silently to the problem of bounced checks. "Have you been paid anything?"

"No, but I haven't sent them a bill yet. I hope I'll be paid in full at the end of their run."

"I don't think you have anything to worry about," he said in a soothing fatherly voice.

The hook was set. Didi began to reel him in.

Still using that half-frightened voice that makes older males buttery, she asked: "Do you have any other professional dealings with the circus?"

Charles Dunlop laughed. "You make the term 'professional dealings' sound like a disease."

"Well, I am a veterinarian," she said sweetly.

"There's really nothing to worry about," he reaffirmed. "And as to your question—Yes, we did make some transfers for them."

The back of Didi's neck tensed. She leaned forward just a bit.

"What's a transfer?" she asked.

He smiled as if it was quite common for young women to be ignorant of banking terms, just like they were usually ignorant of automotive terms. "Well, Didi, when those animals got sick, the circus management asked us to deposit money in an escrow account in Bangkok. In case they needed replacement animals to be flown over quickly."

"But you said the circus opened a small account."

"Oh, they provided us with the additional funds."

"Given the prices of Asian elephants and Bengal tigers," Didi mused, "it must have been a great deal of money transferred."

Charles Dunlop realized he had gone too far in his efforts to reduce Didi's anxieties. The visor of appropriateness slipped down over his handsome face.

"This is really privileged information, Didi. I'm not authorized to discuss it with anyone. Believe me, you don't have anything to worry about as far as your salary goes."

Didi stood to shake hands. Then she walked out of the bank, her nerve endings jangling like one of their alarms.

The Hillsbrook Diner was not yet crowded with the lunch trade. But Didi was happy that Allie had specified the back dining room, which was always empty until the front filled up. She didn't feel like making small talk with even the few people who greeted her. She didn't feel like inquiring into the health of their goats, sows, bulls, calves, bitches—whom she had treated.

It wasn't that she didn't love their beasts; it wasn't that she didn't worry over them . . . it was simply that at the moment her mind was on crime. Ugly, soul-snatching, body dismembering crime.

In fact, she was so deep into thoughts of things criminal that she didn't see Allie approach. Only the weight of his body being seated got her attention.

"Got it!" he said with explosive enthusiasm. His face was wreathed in a Christmas grin. He pushed the piece of paper across the table to her. It was a small piece of white paper that had been ripped haphazardly from a notebook.

"Their last three bookings!" Allie announced.

Didi read the names: Wilmington, Delaware; Rocky Mount, North Carolina; Florence, South Carolina.

"Their route has been due north," Allie noted.

Didi nodded. Allenbach had lied well, concocting a totally bogus west to east route for the circus. But why?

"Are you sure about this itinerary, Allie?"

"Permits don't lie."

Didi folded the paper and placed it into her jacket pocket.

"What did Dunlop say?" Allie asked.

"His bank made transfers for the circus to Thailand."

"What kind of transfers?"

"Money."

"How much?"

"Dunlop wouldn't tell me but it had to be a lot. It was supposedly for the purchase and shipment of circus animals."

"Well, that's logical, Didi."

"Too damn logical, Allie!"

The waitress brought menus.

"Besides, Allie, how could a small circus produce such large amounts of cash suddenly?"

"But Dunlop didn't tell you how much was transferred."

"It wasn't lunch money or he would have told me."

Didi began to study the menu. It was time, she realized, to make her move. She could depend on no one. She could trust no one. Not those in the circus, not those on the periphery of the circus, not those outside the circus completely. Only she and they knew what was going on. But who was the "they"? Someone. In the circus. Maybe several someones. She had the cow by the tail. She knew that. All she had to do was hold on tight.

She put the menu down. She said to Allie: "I have to get back to the house for a few minutes. Can you wait for me here? Just order and eat."

"What happened? An emergency?"

"Something like that."

"Sure. I'll wait."

"And when I come back I'd like to see May Dunlop."

Allie's face registered his befuddlement. "What for?"

Didi took out the unicorn pin. "To return this," she said innocently.

"Come on, Didi. I'm no fool. You're up to something. What's going on?"

"I just want to go to the Dunlop house."

"But why?"

"Take me there, Allie. I promise to be good. I promise not to cause any trouble." Her sarcasm was heavy.

"You're looking for something in the house, right?"

"What you don't know, Allie, won't hurt you." She pressed his arm tenderly, slipped out of the booth and was gone. Allie picked up the menu wearily. But he was hungry.

Trent Tucker and Charlie Gravis were clearly uncomfortable. They had never been invited into Didi's bedroom before. Or into that room when it had been her mother's bedroom. In addition, Miss Quinn was acting a little strange, unfolding maps and flinging them all about.

"Sit down! Sit down! You're making me nervous!" Didi finally shouted at them.

Gingerly, they sat down on the two beautiful matched rocking chairs by the bedroom windows . . . the windows from which one could see the pine forest.

Didi then crouched between them, the road map finally unfolded completely on the floor.

Taking a Magic Marker, she drew a large primitive star next to a spot on the map.

"This is Wilmington, Delaware," she said.

Then another star.

"This is Rocky Mount, North Carolina."

Then another.

"And this is Florence, South Carolina."

Charlie and Trent watched dumbly. From time to time they sneaked a look at each other, as if, perhaps, the other knew what the hell was going on. The other didn't.

"You can make Wilmington way before dinnertime if you leave now. Then on to Rocky Mount; then Florence; then directly back here."

Didi left the map, moved quickly to a drawer, and returned with a white envelope.

She handed it to Charlie. "Here's three hundred dollars in twenties. Use it for gas, tolls, and to eat. No motels. No sleeping out. Time is important. Just change off when one of you gets tired driving. You'll be taking my jeep. I'll make do with Trent's pickup until you get back."

She refolded the map. "For the first leg of the trip, just make believe you're going to Philadelphia. Turn off at Princeton and pick up I-95. Then it's straight as an arrow to Wilmington. No lights. No traffic." She handed Charlie the map. She handed Trent Tucker the keys to the jeep.

Then there was a long silence.

"This is all very nice, Miss Quinn," Charlie finally said in a wry voice. "Me and Trent wouldn't mind taking a nice long drive in your pretty red car. But, Miss Quinn . . . it would be nice to know why we're driving to those places . . . and what we're supposed to do once we get there."

Didi hit the side of her head with her own hand in exasperation at her stupidity. She had been so rushed for time and so intent on the maps and the cash that she had totally forgotten to explain their mission.

"I'm sorry, Charlie. Here's all you have to know. The three cities on your route were the last locations played by our friendly circus. Once you get to each place I want you to gather every existing newspaper clipping pertaining to the circus . . . no matter what the story's about . . . no matter how trivial it seems to you. Use the library. Use the newspapers' own files. Use the visitors bureau. Use the mayor's office. I don't care. But find something on the circus in each place. Anything."

"Okay, Miss Quinn. Trent and I will be ready to leave in an hour or so."

"No, Charlie. You leave now."

"You mean, right now, Miss Quinn?"

"Yes, Charlie. Now! I mean, you walk out of this

room right now with Trent. You walk down the stairs. You walk out the front door. You get into the jeep. You drive. Now!"

Muttering, the two men left Didi's bedroom.

"Have a good trip!" she called out brightly after them. There was no response.

May Dunlop was in the stable behind the large house. It was a three-stall stable but there was only one horse in residence currently.

"Hello!" May said enthusiastically when she saw Allie round the bend of the door. Then she saw Didi and her manner became more sedate. But she kept on brushing the horse with wide swinging strokes.

Allie introduced May Dunlop and Didi again.

"I've heard of you," May said. "You take care of Vic Tanner's show horses, don't you?"

"Yes. In Cold Springs," Didi replied.

"It's a small world," said May.

Didi stepped back to look at the horse May was grooming. It was a large bay thoroughbred gelding—at least seventeen hands high. Very large.

Obviously, it had once been a magnificent animal. But now the aging process had taken over and was accelerating.

"How old is he?" Didi asked.

May put the brush down and blew into the horse's ear affectionately.

"Big Mike is eighteen now. Of course his name is not really Big Mike. It's Venice of Dreams."

"He's out of the Doge's line?" Didi asked.

"Yes. He surely is. And Big Mike and I have been together a long time. In fact, we retired together . . . Isn't that right, Big Mike? Ten long years ago. Big Mike and I were entered in the Puissance Class at Ox Ridge. We made the jump-off. They raised the wall to seven feet. Big Mike stopped. I went over his back into the wall. Broke my collarbone. Lost four teeth. And Big Mike and I never jumped again."

She blew into Big Mike's face. He pulled his head back.

"But you'd like to jump again, wouldn't you?" May said to him. She reached into her jacket and brought out half an apple. Big Mike munched it delicately.

"He doesn't like to be turned out in cold weather. So I just brush him a lot."

She looked at Didi and Allie suddenly, with great intensity. "What does it really matter that I brush him now?"

This woman, Didi thought, is aging beautifully. But she cannot bear to watch her horse grow old. It was a phenomenon that all vets were quite familiar with.

Allie was growing restive with the horse talk. "Didi found another of those pins," he said to May. Then he held out his hand. Didi reached into her pocket, took out the pin, bypassed Allie's hand and gave it directly to May Dunlop. The older woman exhibited little surprise and less happiness at the recovery.

"It was a sudden passion years ago," she explained, holding the pin as if it were not hers. "I had this desire to collect everything that portrayed unicorns in any fashion—pins, buttons, books, paintings, reproductions of tapestries. Now it all seems so stupid. And it makes it more absurd that those children stole them on their spree."

"It wasn't children," Allie said, "and they may not have been drunk. It was people from that circus. At least we think it was. Didi found the pin on the bridle of one of their ponies."

"Sadder still," May said.

"Mrs. Dunlop, may I use one of your bathrooms?" Didi interjected.

May Dunlop pointed toward the house. "Just in from the back door of the house. The door's open."

Didi walked off. Allie stared after her anxiously. He hoped she had enough sense not to do anything stupid—like search the house. He hoped she really had to go to the bathroom. But he doubted it.

He turned back to May Dunlop. She was looking at him in a strange manner. For a moment, Allie had the distinct impression that she wanted to brush him down. But then she started in on Big Mike again.

Allie watched her work, keeping one eye on the house. May was humming a song as she worked. It was vaguely familiar to Allie but he couldn't recall the title. He saw that May had pinned the unicorn on Big Mike's halter. Allie grinned—from a little pony to a big pony.

Then Didi came sauntering back to the stable. Allie felt better. How much damage could she have done in the short time she was in the Dunlop house? Not much.

The three of them made small talk for about five minutes. Then Didi and Allie formally took their leave. May Dunlop thanked them for returning the pin. She thanked them for their visit. She said that Big Mike enjoyed their company—he was lonely.

As they headed toward the car, Allie said, "I was worried you were going to do something you weren't supposed to do."

"You worry a lot, don't you, Allie?"

"When I'm with certain people," he retorted.

"Well, rest easy. All I did was make a local phone call. Then I unscrewed the receiver and took out the listening device the Shelty Sisters had installed there."

Allie stared incredulously at the small aluminum and wire object that Didi was dangling between her two fingers.

"Since this definitely is your jurisdiction, Officer Voegler," she said sarcastically, "I really think you ought to check the premises of those other fake robberies. Don't you? Because that's what they were. Fake robberies."

Chapter 14

Didi sat in one of the rockers in her bedroom. The house was frigid. She had one wool throw around her shoulders and a smaller one around her legs. It was nine minutes past midnight and she wasn't even close to sleep.

She was tense, agitated, her mind racing. Luck had been with her in the Dunlop house. She had just unscrewed the damn telephone and there it was. If it had been a very sophisticated device, she knew she never would have found it.

But she guessed right that *something* would be there. The chain of disclosure had just pulled her along. First the unicorn pin on the pony bridle . . . then the admission by Charles Dunlop that he had transferred large amounts of circus money to Thailand. It had to be something on the wrong side of the law even though the mere transfer of money abroad was not a crime. And the circus had "bugged" Dunlop to make sure he wasn't on to them . . . or perhaps to monitor his conversations with third parties. If a deal was possibly shady, a worried Dunlop would discuss it at home, not in the bank.

Whatever it was—and whether or not Dunlop was a conspirator—it was at the center of the horror.

But the chain had now stopped adding links. The corticosteroids and the elephant book left in the car and the name SIRI seemed to be dead ends.

She desperately needed another link to keep the chain building. She knew she was close to the truth.

Didi leaned back in her chair and rotated her neck to loosen the tightness.

How many were dead now? Ti Nolan. Tran Van Minh. Linda Septiem. Were there others no one knew about? Who were the assassins? The Shelty Sisters? Hardly. Or maybe Allenbach? Or Lothar Strauss? The sword swallower? Those silent and menacing trapeze artists? All of them? None of them? Where did Ti Nolan's animal-rights activism come in? Did it mean anything? Was there another entire aspect of the circus that she had missed . . . that she still wasn't able to identify? Wrong diagnosis? Wrong treatment?

She wanted some of Mrs. Tunney's cocoa. But it was too late for that. She wrapped the throw tighter around her shoulders.

The night was enveloping her. She dreaded insomnia in this bedroom because when she couldn't sleep, memories of her mother began to flood over her. Didi hadn't changed the room one iota and every object, every tint of color had her mother's fingerprints on it. She twisted in the chair to ease the pressure on her aching neck.

Suddenly a light flashed in the darkness outside. At first she thought it was only the beams from a passing car on the road the house fronted.

But the lights grew wider. And then she could hear an engine. Someone was pulling up in front of the house. It could be only one thing, she realized: someone with a very sick animal, probably a house dog or cat, who was just too panicked to call first. Or it could have been a motorist who had hit a deer or a stray dog on the road and then picked up the wounded animal and was bringing it in for help.

Didi threw the blankets off, flung on her big storm coat, and rushed downstairs. She unlatched the front door and stepped into the freezing night.

There was no stranger with a wounded animal.

Charlie Gravis and Trent Tucker were climbing out of her red jeep.

Her anger flared. She clenched her fists. They had been given an assignment. It was simple. Why couldn't they carry it out? What the hell were they doing back in Hillsbrook only twelve hours after they'd left!

"What's going on, Charlie?" Didi shouted at them as they approached.

"Now, now, Miss Quinn, calm down," an out of breath Charlie counseled. He raised his hands in a gesture of submission or perhaps surrender and then stood still. It was Trent Tucker who said: "We found something in Wilmington that Charlie figured you needed right away. So we forgot about the other cities and just headed on home . . . as fast as we could."

Didi led them into her part of the house and up to her room. Charlie sat down heavily on one of the chairs. Trent Tucker fumbled with a brown paper bag under his coat. He finally extricated it.

Didi switched the big light on by the bed. "Here!" she said impatiently. "Put it down here!"

Trent emptied the contents onto the bed. There were two newspapers.

Didi bent down and opened the first newspaper. She stared at the front page blankly. At first she could not believe what she was seeing. She shook her head. Then she sat down on the bed and held the paper in her lap.

The front page of the newspaper contained a story about a young woman vet who was treating one of the circus's sick elephants. The vet's name was Marjorie Browder. The elephant was called Gorgeous.

It was incredible. It was almost the same story that had appeared in the Hillsbrook newspaper with Didi as the healing protagonist.

She grabbed the other paper. It was the same Wilmington paper, dated a week later.

This time the story was about a sick Bengal tiger named Agatha and the same woman vet.

Didi buried her face in her hands.

"Are you okay, Miss Quinn?" Charlie asked, concerned.

Didi motioned with her hand that she was fine. She stood up and took in an enormous breath. Things were happening very fast now in Didi's head. The links were reappearing.

"You both did good," she said quietly, her voice trembling slightly. She placed the newspapers back in the bag.

"We're going to the circus," she said.

"Now?" Trent Tucker asked.

"Now! Tell me, Charlie, do you still have that shotgun?"

"The one you told me to get rid of, Miss Quinn?"

"Yes, that one, Charlie."

"Well, Miss Quinn, to be honest, I forgot all about it. It just slipped my mind. If you want me to get rid of it, I surely will."

"Get it, Charlie. Bring some shells. Put it in the jeep. Now, Charlie."

Charlie ambled off. "I'll meet you in the jeep in five minutes, Trent," Didi said. The young man left the room quickly, his face charged with the excitement of it all—nighttime visits, shotguns, long drives.

Didi looked wildly about the bedroom for a moment. Then she rushed to the dresser, opened the bottom drawer and violently flung stacks of papers and old letters out onto the floor, falling to her knees and searching frantically through the debris.

Then she sat back on her heels with a cry of triumph. In her hand was an old subpoena with which she had once been served; she had been called upon to testify in one of those bizarre dog-bite cases. In this one, one dairy farmer had sued another dairy farmer because the latter's dog had bitten the ear of a calf belonging to the former, causing permanent psychological damage according to the former. It had the word SUBPEONA writ large in ugly letters and uglier ink. It had a big red seal. She stuffed it into her back pocket, grabbed the bag with the newspapers, and rushed down the stairs. In spite of the cold her face was flushed.

They drove fast on the empty roads, making the trip in a bit more than thirty minutes.

Didi swerved onto the circus grounds. The realization of what had happened hit all the jeep's occupants at the same moment.

The circus grounds were empty.

The trucks and the trailers and the tents and the animals and the people were all gone.

Didi climbed out of the jeep. The others followed. The scene dazed her, confused her. The circus people seemed to have left in a great hurry. Mounds of garbage and discarded ropes and light bulbs and crushed cartons littered the ground.

"You can tell by the tire tracks that they headed west . . . probably toward the Thruway," Trent Tucker said.

Didi walked slowly about, in a half circle, as if people and animals would reappear if one was patient.

"What do we do now?" Charlie Gravis asked.

"Stop the bleeding," Didi responded automatically. The realization of the absurdity of her own remark brought Didi out of her daze. "No, Charlie, there is something we can do and we are going to do it now. I want you to drive to Allie Voegler's place."

"You mean his home?"

"Yes. He lives in the village, in that small building right next to the bookstore. Second floor rear."

"You want me to wake him up now, Miss Quinn?"

"Yes. The minute you arrive there. Wake him up. Tell him where we are. Tell him the circus has pulled up stakes. Tell him I have proof of multiple murders! Tell him to get Lieutenant Jacks of the state police and bring him here. Tell him he must act fast. Do you have all that, Charlie? Good. Trent and I will wait here. Leave the shotgun with us!"

It was a strange conference. Three cars were parked facing each other and defining a small circle. Their front lights illuminated the circle.

One of the cars was the red jeep. Trent Tucker and Charlie Gravis sat shivering in it.

One of the cars was Allie Voegler's unmarked police vehicle.

One of the cars was a New York State police cruiser with a fully uniformed, unforgiving trooper sitting at the wheel.

In the circle, in the car lights, in the cold, stood Allie Voegler, Lieutenant Jacks, and Didi.

"Let me get this straight. You want me to stop the circus in transit on the highway?" Jacks asked, speaking to Didi but staring accusingly at Allie.

Didi had picked up on the animosity between Allie Voegler and Lieutenant Jacks. She realized it shouldn't have surprised her. Local police tend to dislike state troopers because of their showy uniforms and because they seem to get all the publicity. Yet, Jacks and Voegler seemed very much alike to Didi, although the former was of a different generation. They even dressed the same in civilian clothes—flannel shirts and knit ties.

She had to make her points but she had to be careful. It was a mine field of conflicting jurisdictions. Above all, she had to get Jacks to order the circus to be stopped now.

"There are murderers traveling with that circus," Didi said.

"Who have they murdered?" Jacks countered.

"Ti Nolan and Linda Septiem."

"We investigated those deaths. We consider them tragic accidents."

"They were murdered because they discovered the truth about the circus."

"And what is that truth?"

"It is a money-laundering operation."

"For whom do they launder this money?"

"I don't know."

"What do you know?" Jacks's question was laced with cynicism.

"I know that they follow a certain procedure in each city they play. They open a small bank account. Then several of their animals get ill. They ask the bank officials to wire large sums of money to Thailand to insure that replacement animals will be shipped if the ill ones die. The animals recover. They move on and begin the game all over again."

She could see that Jacks was beginning to squirm. She continued. "To make sure that nothing goes wrong, they conduct fake break-ins at the houses of the bank officials who have made the transfers. The purpose of these break-ins is to place listening devices."

She moved close to Lieutenant Jacks and opened her fist. "This was found in Charles Dunlop's house. And pins stolen during the fake break-in were found in the possession of certain circus performers."

Jacks picked up the small listening device and turned it over in his hand. Then he dropped it back into Didi's palm.

"What else do you have?" he asked.

She handed him the newspapers. He studied them. "A remarkable coincidence," he admitted. "Almost exactly like the stories about you."

"Yes, remarkable," Didi affirmed. She pulled the

vial of corticosteroids out of her jacket and handed it to him. "The animals were made sick. Corticosteroids are immunosuppressive and fevers are often a side effect. That is probably what led Ti Nolan to her death. She found out about the steroids. She tried to stop it."

Lieutenant Jacks shook the vial. Then he gave it back.

"Do you have any evidence that the two women were murdered? Do you have any evidence that the money transferred overseas came from illicit activity?"

"Not yet," Didi agreed. "But I can get it from that circus caravan. I can get it now . . . if you stop it."

He seemed to be wavering. "There's only one circus performer I must speak to," Didi said. "There's only one who will talk. There's only one who can end this horror."

Allie Voegler spoke for the first time. To Jacks. "They are probably traveling on invalid permits because they closed down four days early. They are also traveling with dangerous animals. Any convoy can be stopped to insure security of the public."

Lieutenant Jacks stared from Allie to Didi and then back. As if there were a conspiracy against him.

"Well," he said slowly, "first let's see if we can find them on the radio."

He walked back to the cruiser. Didi saw him talking to the uniformed trooper at the wheel.

"Are you cold?" Allie asked.

"A bit."

"I have an extra sweater in the trunk."

"Don't need it. Thanks," Didi replied, and then waved to Trent Tucker and Charlie Gravis, huddling in the red jeep. They did not wave back.

"Can I look at those Wilmington papers?" Allie asked. Didi thrust them into his hand. He was making small talk, she realized, and she wasn't interested in small talk at all.

"If you're right about all this, Didi, then you have to admit these characters are pretty slick."

Didi saw Lieutenant Jacks walking slowly back into the circle of headlights. She snatched the papers from Allie.

This time he looked straight at Didi.

"Okay. We know where they are. They're on the Thruway. Heading north. Between Kingston and Saugerties. We should be able to reach them in less than an hour. I'll lead. Let Officer Voegler follow me. And you follow him."

The wild ride was over. The convoy had been stopped in the right lane of the Thruway. Warning lights had been set out behind the last trailer to detour oncoming traffic safely.

Didi had never before pushed her jeep to those speeds: 80 miles an hour. And the effort had exhausted her and frightened Charlie Gravis. Their three-car convoy had pulled off the road onto the embankment, resting in the shadow of the larger vehicles.

Lieutenant Jacks approached the jeep. He was blowing into his hands to keep warm. "Okay," he said, "we're going to make this fast. Tell me who you want."

"His name is Lothar Strauss. He trains the Bengal tigers."

Jacks nodded. "I'll bring him here. I'll give you fifteen minutes with him. And that'll be it. My trooper is going to cite them for several violations. Their trailers are in miserable condition."

Didi watched Lieutenant Jacks head toward Allenbach's trailer. She felt, oddly, like Salome, sending one of Herod's captains to bring her the head of John the Baptist. The analogy was all skewed, she realized, but that was the way she felt. It was probably because of the phrase Jacks had used: "I'll bring him here."

Then she asked Charlie Gravis and Trent Tucker to leave the jeep. To move into Allie Voegler's car, temporarily. Grumbling, they complied.

She sat alone, in the jeep, waiting. It was possible that she was going to have to do some ugly things . . . some dishonest things. And she steeled herself to that eventuality. When her mother was frightened, she used to recite Edgar Allan Poe's poem "The Bells." It calmed her. It gave her strength. Didi had always found it odd that her mother, who was a profoundly Christian woman, would use that poem for spiritual strength. Why not one of the Psalms? But it didn't matter anyway. Didi had never learned the words. And when her mother had recited it out loud, it had always given her a headache.

Then she saw the figure of Lieutenant Jacks approaching, followed by Lothar Strauss.

Jacks opened the passenger side of the jeep and waited for Lothar to climb in. The cat trainer hesitated as if he had an option. But there was none. He climbed in. Jacks slammed the door shut.

Didi turned in her seat so she could face him. He didn't look at her. He kept his face straight ahead.

"I know you put the book and drugs into the car."

He didn't say a word.

"I know it was you, Lothar. There were not many people who knew about corticosteroids . . . who knew what they could do. There was Ti Nolan and she was dead. There was Tran Van Minh and he was dead. There were the Shelty Sisters but they do not use any medicines for their ponies. So that left you, Lothar. Aren't I right, Lothar?"

He still didn't speak. She could see the muscles on his neck bunching up. He seemed to be having trouble breathing correctly.

"And the picture book confirmed it, Lothar. It was a book that Ti Nolan had given you. Wasn't it? A gift she had made to you while you were lovers or after the affair ended."

Lothar Strauss turned toward her suddenly and said in a loud voice: "I don't know what you're talking about. I don't know anything about an elephant book or a drug. I don't know anything about a car."

Didi continued to speak in a friendly, almost exploratory fashion, as if they were engaged on a quest together. "A lot is clear to me now, Lothar. How the bank accounts were opened. How the animals were made ill. How the papers were contacted for this remarkable human-interest story. How the ill animals were used as an excuse for the money transfers to Thailand. How Ti and Linda Septiem died because they either discovered the whole operation, or more likely, just discovered the drugging of the animals and threatened to report it.

"And I even think I know, Lothar, why you dumped those pieces of evidence into the car."

For the first time since he had entered the jeep she saw a crack in his armor. He seemed to wince and shift his body uncomfortably.

"You're a kind man, Lothar. You're not evil. Whatever this circus is up to, you went along because the money was good. Right, Lothar? But then Tran was ordered to get Ti Nolan out of the way because she was too inquisitive . . . because she was taking her animal-rights advocacy too seriously. And you loved her as much as Tran did, didn't you, Lothar? And then came the night of Linda Septiem's murder. Probably Ti Nolan had confided in her about the corticosteroids. Maybe she knew even more. What was it, Lothar? They told you to leave the cage unlocked. And you didn't want to participate in what was going to happen. You didn't want to jeopardize your Bengals. So you were afraid to act and afraid not to act. You couldn't leave and you couldn't stay. So you followed orders and at the same time you eased your conscience by offering up some clue to what was going on."

Suddenly Lothar Strauss grabbed the door handle and tried to get out of the jeep. From the outside, Lieutenant Jacks slammed the door back shut, keeping Lothar within.

"Tell me, Lothar, who is behind all of this. Tell me where the money for those transfers is coming from. Tell me why so many people have died."

The sweat was now pouring down Lothar's face. But he didn't say a word.

Didi stared at him. She would have to do the worst. She had planned for it; but she had hoped it would not be necessary. For a moment she hesitated. All her upbringing and training had taught her to be ethical in any situation. That the end never justifies the means. But they were all awash in a sea of innocent blood.

"Open the glove compartment, Lothar," she said.

He didn't move. She leaned forward and pressed the button. The small door dropped down and the light within went on.

"Do you see what's in there, Lothar?"

She could see him staring at the folded legal document with the word subpoena on it and the garish seal.

"It's for you, Lothar. We are going to take your Bengals. And I'm afraid they're going to be put down."

He became rigid. The tears started to mingle with sweat.

"Save your cats," she whispered urgently. "Tell me!"

He lashed out with one hand, striking her on the mouth. Her head went back against the seat. Then his powerful hands grabbed her around her throat. She tried to scream but the pressure of his hands was too great.

Suddenly the doors of the jeep opened and other hands appeared, dragging him off her, holding him rigid against the seat. She saw Jacks and Allie Voegler. "Are you okay, Didi? Are you okay?" It was Allie speaking to her, from the back of the seat, leaning over, one of his arms still imprisoning Lothar.

She nodded that she was okay. She tasted blood in her mouth. She looked at Lothar. He was fighting Jacks and Voegler. But their grip was too strong.

"Save your cats," she whispered to him through bruised lips.

He seemed to deflate . . . to collapse. He whispered something. She couldn't hear. She motioned to Allie in the back seat to remove his arms from Lothar's neck. Allie did so.

"Faulkner and Runay," he was saying. Faulkner and Runay. As if they were a song-and-dance team.

How bizarre, she thought. The music man and the sword swallower. And Allenbach was their marionette.

"The source of the money, Lothar? Tell me the source of the money." Her voice was pleading. Her hand involuntarily went to the face of the man who had just tried to strangle her. As if he were a sick animal that she was trying to console before treating.

"White elephant," he whispered.

Didi turned away from him. She stared into the darkness of her windshield. Queen Siri . . . she thought . . . the bloody graffiti . . . the queen who was impregnated by a white elephant with a lotus in its trunk.

"The little flags, Lothar? Is that it? The satin flags from Thailand. The bolts of cloth?"

He nodded.

"Where do they keep the bolts, Lothar? Do you know? Can you take us to them?"

He nodded. Didi gestured to Jacks that he should help Lothar out.

They began to walk along the line of the convoy. Huge shadows played about them. A cold wind seemed to perpetually push them away from the convoy. Jacks held Lothar's arm tightly. Allie held

Didi's arm, afraid she would fall. But Didi was strong again. She needed no help.

Lothar led them to one of the elephant trailers. They climbed inside. The two elephants eyed them nonchalantly. Lothar pointed to one of the storage bins along the wall of the trailer. Allie pulled it open. There among a welter of performance trappings stood three large bolts of cloth.

Allie pulled one down and rolled it open on the straw-covered floor.

It was like satin wallpaper. Endless repetitions of the same white elephant theme that could be cut into squares and attached to flag sticks.

Once it was completely unrolled, Lothar took a deep breath and squatted beside the bolt.

His hands went to the stitching along the edges of the bolt . . . a border which gave the fabric enough weight so it would not crinkle in transit.

His fingers moved along the stitching, like a piano player. They all watched fascinated. Then he found something. He stopped, stood up, and pointed down to a specific segment of stitching.

"Cut it open, Allie," Didi said. Allie took out his pocket knife, pulled the small blade open, and slit the seam.

Eight small objects fell out. Rubies. Each one a different size. Each one slightly different in color but in absolutely magnificent red. They were dazzling in the wisps of straw.

Jacks bent down and picked two up, rolling

them in his palm. "These are cut and polished. These are finished stones."

He bent down again and let the stones roll back onto the floor. "Ingenious, very ingenious," he marveled. "Bolts of flag cloth are shipped to the circus in the U.S. With the smuggled rubies. The circus distributes them throughout the U.S. on its travels. The money is then transferred back to Thailand, the source of the smuggled rubies. Ingenious."

Didi turned away from the beautiful gems. She felt sickened. She felt cheapened. So many dead for those stupid little ornaments.

She walked deeper into the trailer toward the elephants. One of them reached out to her with her trunk. She realized it was Gorgeous. The powerful trunk rested on her arm, waiting for a snack. Didi laughed. "I'm sorry, Gorgeous. I have nothing for you." The elephant turned her full face toward Didi. "But, if I bring you some lotus flowers to munch, Gorgeous, will you let me ride you?" The elephant did not answer.

Don't miss the next
Deirdre Quinn Nightingale
mystery,
DR. NIGHTINGALE GOES
TO THE DOGS,
coming from Signet
in February 1995.

Didi stood up and stepped away from Lucifer. Lucifer was a six and a half month old Duroc pig. Of the breed they used to call Jersey Reds—hearty, fast-growing, intelligent.

She stripped the examining gloves from her hands and let them drop to the ground.

Deirdre Quinn Nightingale, D.V.M., was angry. Very, very angry.

She stared at Ledeen, the man who owned the pig. Then she stared at Charlie Gravis, her geriatric veterinary assistant, who had persuaded her to come out to examine Lucifer.

"Do you mind, Mr. Ledeen, if I confer privately with my assistant?" she asked with exaggerated formality.

"Hell, no," said Ledeen. He was a tall, gangly man with a ponytail. He wore a flannel shirt beneath his overalls even though it was a warm day. Except for his neatly kept goatee, his face was clean shaven and heavily scarred. His eyes were deep set and constantly moving.

"Thank you, Mr. Ledeen," Didi replied and walked out of the makeshift pen, motioning for Charlie Gravis to follow.

When they were out of Ledeen's earshot, Didi stripped off her weathered jumpsuit, revealing a handsome pale yellow dress with a high collar and long sleeves. She folded the dirty outer garment carefully.

"Are you feeling okay, Charlie?" she asked.

"Just fine, miss," he replied.

"You *do* know what day it is, don't you, Charlie?"

"Yes, miss. Your birthday. June 30."

"Right. And you *do* know what is going on today, don't you, Charlie? In about an hour or so."

"A party, miss. Your birthday party."

"But it's not just any birthday party—right, Charlie? It's the first party of any kind that I've given since I came back to Hillsbrook. It's the first time our neighbors and friends have come to the house since my mother died. Isn't that right, Charlie?"

"Right, miss."

"So it's not just a silly old birthday party, is it, Charlie? It's something special. It's something I'm doing because of a whole lot of hurt and pride in my heart, Charlie. It's about my mother. Do you understand that, Charlie?"

"Yes, miss."

"And we've all been very busy preparing for this. And I still have to get the ice and I have to pick up

Mary Hyndman at her place and take her to the party because she's too infirm now to drive."

"I know all that, miss."

"If you know all that, Charlie, why did you get me out here on this fool's errand? You said it was an emergency. What kind of emergency, Charlie? Where is the emergency? Is the world going to come to an end because Lucifer is just not interested in the two sows in heat that Ledeen penned on either side of him? Is that your emergency, Charlie? Is that why you dragged me all the way out here?"

"He was very upset on the phone. He was calling from the gas station," Charlie explained. And then he added, "And he's kin."

"Kin!"

"Yes, miss. Kin."

"A twelfth cousin on your uncle's side? Is that it, Charlie?" Didi clenched and unclenched her fists and stared down at her shoes, which she had forgotten to change. They were covered with mud.

It was futile to get angry with Charlie, she thought, but she couldn't help herself. Kin! All four of the nice misfits she had inherited from her mother—Charlie and Mrs. Tunney and Abigail and Trent Tucker—were all "kin." Whatever that meant. Sooner or later everyone was everyone else's cousin. She stared past Charlie to the obviously unhappy Mr. Ledeen. She could tell he was poor and desperate. But everyone who lived on the Ridge was poor and desperate. They all lived, like

Mr. Ledeen, in trailers set up on cinder blocks without hot water or electricity or phones. The Ridge was Hillsbrook's Tobacco Road. As Hillsbrook itself had become more affluent, more suburban, the Ridge had grown poorer. People of the Ridge raised pigs to survive—to eat.

Didi walked over to Mr. Ledeen, who did a double take when he noticed her outfit. He was confused by her transformation from farm hand to belle of the ball.

"There's nothing the matter with Lucifer," she said simply.

"The hell there ain't," Ledeen snapped. "He ain't gruntin', he ain't salivatin', and there's two pretty young things on either side of him all hot to go. Don't tell me there ain't nothing the matter with him."

"Mr. Ledeen!" Didi said sharply, assuming her role as Dr. Quinn, the ultimate authority on all things animal. "I have examined your boar very carefully. There is no brucellosis or osteomalacia or arthritis. The testicles, epididymides, and scrotum are fine. Locomotor function is fine. You just have to be patient with Lucifer. Some boars achieve sexual maturity later than others. It's as simple as that."

"He's old enough, he is. Six and a half months. I ain't never had a boar who couldn't do it at six and a half months. But it ain't a question of him not being able to do it—he don't *want* to do it."

"It is quite common for boars to remain sexually

immature until they are eight months of age, Mr. Ledeen. In fact, there are some large-scale pig farming operations that won't use a boar before he reaches eight months."

Ledeen shook his head stubbornly. "No. You gotta take a whaddayacallit—a semen sample. Send it to the lab. Gotta do that. Something bad is wrong with Lucifer."

Didi glared at the man. She was astonished at his arrogance. Everybody knew that Ledeen didn't have a dime to pay for anything. Didi knew this was going to be a free visit, that it would be useless even to send Ledeen a bill. And now he wanted complicated procedures and lab work done for a pig that was perfectly healthy.

"I am going to give that some consideration, Mr. Ledeen," Didi said, "but right now I have another client waiting."

"Charlie!" Ledeen shouted. "This is no way to treat kin."

Didi struggled to keep her cool.

"Tell me, Mr. Ledeen," she said, "are there any heritable defects in Lucifer's line?"

"Say what?"

"Did his daddy have a scrotal hernia?"

"His daddy was a damn tiger."

"Then Lucifer too will become one, no doubt—in forty-five days or so. And there is no need whatever to evaluate his semen, Mr. Ledeen. Now, good day!"

She walked briskly back to the red Jeep. Charlie Gravis fell into step behind her.

"Do we get ice first?" Charlie asked once they were on the road.

"No. We get Mary Hyndman first, Charlie." Didi spoke gently, having decided not to broach the subject of Ledeen's unamorous pig ever again.

She drove more slowly than usual because she was heading toward Mary's cottage without locational confidence. The way was not really clear. It had been nine months since she had gone to see Mary, and that was the first and last time she had ever been to the cottage. It had been a professional visit: to put down Mary's last remaining German shepherd—a bitch named Raymonda who could no longer see or walk.

Mary herself had already become infirm. She got around on a walker. But, after all, Mary was close to ninety. Didi had sent her an invitation to the birthday party but had never expected a reply. The reply had come, however, and promptly. Yes, Mary had said, she would like to attend—if someone could come and pick her up, because she could no longer manage the car.

Everyone was astonished that Mary Hyndman wanted to come to the party under any circumstances. She had been a virtual recluse since her husband's death ten years ago.

"I remember that beat-up old sycamore tree," Didi noted. She accelerated, now sure of the way.

They were close to the cottage. Didi felt good. It

was a rare pleasure to see Mary. And the old woman would understand the importance of the party. She was a wise lady. Didi's mother had always confided in Mary. Everyone had, until she withdrew from all her friends.

Mary was tall—almost six feet—with a kind of hunched back and a beautiful face. Her hair was always long and loose. Her husband had been affiliated with one of those international foundations that dispensed disaster aid. He and Mary were always off to Malaysia or northeast Brazil or Ethiopia after an earthquake or war.

Mary was also a legendary gardener and in the early 1960s had published a book, *The Complete Garden*, in which she had argued that flowers and vegetables should be grown together in the same soil. The exquisite photographs and detailed instructions in the book then demonstrated how to plant and manage such a garden.

"Right here!" Didi said happily and turned the Jeep off the main road and onto the narrow dirt path that led to Mary Hyndman's place.

"Look out!" Charlie yelled.

Didi swerved at the same time an oncoming green station wagon swerved. Luckily the swerves were coordinated.

Both vehicles squealed to a stop.

"Sorry!" Didi called out to the large redheaded and red bearded man behind the wheel.

Then she saw the M.D. plates on his car.

Quickly she climbed out of the jeep and approached him. "Is Mary okay?"

"She's fine," the physician answered. "She had a fall. But nothing's broken."

"What happened to Dr. Fisk?" Didi asked, remembering the name of the doctor that Mary had spoken about during that sad visit when Raymonda was put down.

"He's on vacation. I'm covering for him. I'm Dr. Purdy, from Dover Plains."

He started his engine. "You ought to make a wider turn next time so you can see if another vehicle is coming down the path," he counseled pompously.

Didi just nodded. He was right.

"By the way," Dr. Purdy called as he drove off, "I left the front door open so the puppy could go in and out. Those were Mrs. Hyndman's instructions." He turned onto the main road and vanished from sight.

Didi was taken aback for a moment. Had she heard right—*a puppy?* She turned to Charlie, who was still in his seat and obviously still a little shaken from the near collision.

"Did he say Mary had a puppy?"

"That's what I heard, miss."

Didi got back into the Jeep, shaking her head. "Tell me, Charlie, how she can manage a puppy when she can't even manage herself?"

Charlie only shrugged.

Didi parked by the fenced-in, overgrown garden

that adjoined Mary's cottage. She could smell the radishes and scallions growing through the weeds.

As she headed for the front door, which the good doctor had indeed left open for the sake of the puppy, Didi laughed a little wickedly and pointed at the garden fence.

"Look, Charlie," she said, "the woman is past ninety and she still makes a better scarecrow than you."

The big, brooding figure hanging on the garden fence certainly was an impressive scarecrow. With an enormous straw hat. A threatening totem to keep all manner of predators away from the delicate vegetables.

Didi started to climb the three-step porch.

"Wait a minute, miss!"

It was Charlie who had shouted.

"Wait for what?" Didi asked.

"That ain't no scarecrow."

Didi blinked the sun out of her eyes. She began to run toward the hatted object. Then she turned away, quickly, violently.

Charlie was right. It wasn't a scarecrow. That was Mary Hyndman hanging on the fence. And there were three small holes in the center of her forehead. Neat, well-placed bullet holes.

And be sure to read the first book in the Dr. Nightingale series: DR. NIGHTINGALE COMES HOME

Veterinarian Deirdre Quinn Nightingale practices in rural New York and is currently trying to diagnose the strange malady her neighbor's dairy goats have come down with. She is quite familiar with animal sickness and death, but she embarks on her first investigation of a human death when her good friend and dairy farmer, Dick Obey, is found dead and horribly mutilated. During Deirdre's search for the truth, she discovers that Dick Obey wasn't the kindly man she thought he was and that many people had reason to kill him.

TANTALIZING MYSTERIES